Lette
V is for Victoria

A Day in the Life of Them Vassar Girls Series
Novel   Book I / Volume

A DAY IN THE LIFE OF THEM VASSAR GIRLS

SERIES/NOVEL

BOOK I / VOLUME I

Lette

Dedication/Acknowledgement

My Loves,

As I sit here, this first day of the year 2017 thinking as to what I need to say after literally writing this book in 5 days (started on Christmas Day 2016 while watching my grandchildren play with their toys), I want to make sure that I hit everything and everyone that needs to be acknowledged within this journey. I would like to recognize some people that I feel made this book a reality. To Sabrina Lee Moton, the one who always saw potential in everything that I do and was the first one to say to me that she saw me writing a book and I will be doggone if she was not right. She was the first person to read this particular book besides me and I could not be prouder of the relationship that we have because of this. I love you for believing in me and keeping on my head about finishing this project. To my children, Camari Sr. and Camani, you have both tested me to no ends, especially during the time of me writing this book, but I would not trade any part of my life with you and am so proud to be your mother. You have both grown up to be beautiful people who with the right guidance from God, will always pursue to make the correct decisions within your life to help make you two better individuals individually as well as together. To my grandchildren, Beniaih, Messiah, Fat Fat (Camari Jr.), Ca`Mya and Jediah, to you, I do this all for you, my loves. To my mom, Susan Thompson and my big sister Aleera (Sherry) Thompson, my biggest supporters, I love you to life and would not be the person that I am if it was not for the two of you. The two women in my life (along with my maternal grandmother) who molded my spirit, my spirituality, my moral compass, my compassion and my heart. I love you and I am the strong minded woman that I am because of you. To my family, my grandfather, Abraham Thompson Sr. (1918 – 1994), my grandmother, Mary G. Thompson (Oatney - 1915 – 2011), my uncle Major Capers (1943 – 2005), my aunt Sallie (Ayn) Blackmon (Thompson), my uncle Brother (Abraham Thompson Jr.) and to all of my cousins (1st, 2nd, 3rd and so forth and so on), you make me proud to be in the company that I keep in this family. Because we rock baby!!! No hate, no drama, no lack of love. Just fun, good times, jokes, laughter, respect and pure hilarity. We have always been considered to be one of the nicest, kindest, most respectful and considerate families on this earth by many who know and love us and I am so proud of how we were all raised and how we have raised and are still raising our families to keep up the tradition. Being in this family is such a blessing! Am I my family's keeper? Hell Yeah!!!! To the best friends ever! I have some of the best friends ever! That is all that I can say. I have some of the best friends ever! I cannot name you all but you know who you are (special shout out my angels A. (Rabbit) Thompson (my cuz), R. Granberry, S. Reed (check her out on the book cover), C. Brooks, D. Hayes, J. Barksdale, R. Thornton, L. Alexander, E. Connor, A. Lawrence, M. Mills, G. Harkless, & D. Hu). I love you all and thank you for being my rocks! To "P" (Lol), I thank you for loving me as your friend/confidant during the good times and being there when I needed you, at the time that I needed you but I thank you more for loving me enough to walk away and for not loving me enough, so that we would both finally stop the fight of wanting you to stay. Last but not least, to my Lord and Savior. My God, my God, my God. Thank you for showing me what I needed to see in order to understand this world of mine just a little better. Thank you for the lesson of the friendship, trust, love, loyalty, disloyalty, jealousy, deceit, betrayal, hurt, pain and that everything/everybody is not what it/they seem to be on the surface and for keeping me grounded and humble enough and never letting me be the type of person who changes, except for the better, who I am because of it. Thank you for never ever letting me go to a place beneath my level due to sharp objects constantly being thrown my way. Thank you for the raw emotions that were thrust upon me unexpectedly, which helped me within the process and helped me hone my skills to express things from a place that I would not have ever even sent fit to do if it were not for you. Thank for shaking up my world and showing me the idea of what happiness could be and showing me what it feels like to feel at home. Thank you for letting me know that sometimes it is okay to let my guard down but also at the same time to keep my life guarded. Thank you for keeping me in a place where No One Ever Knows Everything. Thank you for the power of Mystery. Thank you for preparing me for greatness by the lesson of breaking my heart. I would not have been able to come from a place of pureness and understanding if it was not for what I have been through. Thank you for the power of forgiveness. No love lost. No take backs. No regrets. It was all necessary. Thank you for allowing me to be who you set out for me to be. Thank you for enlisting your prayer warriors to always have my back. Thank you for continuing to let me know that it is okay to just be me and excel in my day to day to make sure that I do everything I am meant to do to do right by you. Thank you for the good, the bad and the ugly for without you I am nothing. Thank you for the power of love and thank you for giving me such a big heart and making it always known that I will never change who I am because of what comes my way. Thank you for making me one of the nice girls (Cancer's Rule). I will never change! Lord, I thank you. I thank you. I thank you.

xoxo xoxo

Love,

Lette

Chapter 1

"It's soooo cold in this room," she whispered. The tension was so thick that you could cut it with a big ass knife. They have not seen one another since that faithful day three years ago when she decided that she was not in a place to be able to continue with the relationship as it was. She has always regretted the way that things ended but at the time, she was just not ready to make such a big commitment. It was not until she decided to move on, that it came to her that maybe she was more ready than she even thought that she was. She wondered, *As I sit in this room, trying not to stare at this man, I can't help but to wonder, what if? I have always wondered what may have been if I could have come to the conclusion of a serious commitment. I was scared. I was terrified. I did not know how to take it all in when he asked me to marry him. I was speechless. I did not say no, but my saying nothing at all made it worse. He stood there in front of all of our family and friends, waiting for me to say something and all I could do was stand there in a trance, and stare at him in disbelief of what was going on.* It was so vivid within her memory. *The look on his face was horrifying. I will never forget it. I have cried myself to sleep many a night from just thinking of how I hurt this man who loved me so much, that he took the time to give me a dream proposal in front of all of our family and friends. Now I stand here, shocked, that I am in the same room with him after being invited to my new boss's engagement party.*"

Victoria had only been on the job for a little over three months, but she and her new boss had gotten pretty close within that time. She and Rasha Du'Voe just clicked from the first day they met. Rasha was an island-born beauty who ran the company with class, grace and dignity, but also ruled this male-dominated field with an iron-clad fist. Victoria experienced one of the best interviews ever with her about four months ago when she decided to move back to Detroit after moving away to escape her past two and a half years ago. Interviewing for the position of financial consultant for one of the biggest brokerage firms in the country, it was imperative that she aced it. When she first met Rasha, she was a little intimidated, but they both knew from the start that this was going to be a great pairing. Over the past three months, they have had countless breakfasts, brunches, lunches and dinners discussing how to make the individual departments, as well as the company, flourish and continue to stay within the top rankings in the market. Being one of the most successful Fortune 500 companies in the country, this was one of the greatest moves that Victoria felt she had made so far since coming back into town. Now she sits here at this party feeling like she wanted to sink down into the closest dark corner.

She thought, *God, he looks great.* He was tall, handsome, of a stocky build and had some of the deepest, darkest chocolate smooth skin. *And that dimple.* He had a single dimple on his right cheek. Victoria pondered, "That man was so good to me. Now I stand here like a statue, feeling like if I had the guts, I would walk across this room and tell him that I would like to do nothing more than fall into his arms and let him know that even after all of these years, he still makes me weak in the knees."

Rasha approached Victoria. "Victoria?" She snapped out of it and looked up. "Is everything okay?"

She was so lost in thought; she didn't even know that Rasha had been trying to get her attention for a good minute. "Excuse me?" she replied, a little confused.

Rasha commented, "You did not see me waving at you from across the room?" Victoria, still confused, just stared at her. "Are you ok? You look a little flushed. As if all of the color has left your face. Is everything alright? Do you need to sit down or need some water?"

Still stunned, Victoria replied, "I am okay." He was still laying heavy on her mind. "Sorry. I just thought I saw someone that I knew, but I am okay." Rasha looked a little worried, but she just acted as if she wanted to appear as if she thought that Victoria was okay. She went on to ask Victoria, "Are you enjoying yourself so far?"

She answered, "Why yes. Everything is so beautiful. So lovely."

Rasha was flattered by the compliment, "Aww, thank you so much." She continued talking, but Victoria barely heard a word that she was saying, because she was once again lost in her thoughts. *What is my next move? Do I go over and say hi? He sees me. Why should I go over there? Why has he not come over to speak to me?* She began mentally slapping herself across the head. *Well...I guess not, lady, since you are the one who did the damage. Lord, let me know what to do.*

Rasha brought her back to reality. "I told you that I am determined to find you a man. You are too beautiful of a girl to still be out here single. Girl, look at you. You are killing that suit!" And that she was. Victoria was a curvaceous woman. She stood 5'9" with caramel-colored skin, thick lips, big hips and a bottom that would put Kim K's to shame. Victoria wore a black body suit made of velvet material that silhouetted over every curve of her body. Her hair was pinned in a messy bun, with a Chinese bang, with silver accessories and a pair of six-inch stilettos to die for, completing the look. No one could say that Victoria did not have it going on, not by a long shot. Rasha started scanning the room. "Now where is he?" The person she was searching for finally caught her attention. "Oh, there he is. He is standing over there with my fiancé. I would like to introduce you two, as well as to my Boobie." Victoria thought Rasha's nickname for him was so cute. She claimed it was a combination of calling him her boo-boo and her baby. "I think that you two would really hit it off."

Victoria did not want to meet anyone. She was just not in the mood tonight, especially after seeing her ex. "Rasha, if you don't mind? Not tonight. I am just not in a place to do that in my life right now," she commented.

Rasha grabbed her arm, gave it a gentle squeeze. "Oh come on, give it a chance. I can't take up all of your free time," she joked. Victoria gave a forced chuckle. At that moment, she gestured in the direction of her ex and two of his acquaintances to come their way. Internally, Victoria started to panic. *Oh, no. She can't be...are you serious? Is it one of the guys with him...or worse yet, is she about to try to set me up with my ex? No way is he coming this way. Not like this. I don't want to talk to him like this.* She noticed the look on her ex's face and thought, *God, he looks so good though, but at the same time is looking very strange. As a matter of fact, he is looking very confused.*

Rasha greets them and then reaches out to grab his hand. At that moment, it hit her like a bolt of lightning. There is no way that God would do this to her. Suddenly, she became dizzy and felt the feeling in her legs go limp. "Hey, Boobie, I would like to introduce you to the woman in my life as you say, since she has taken up so many of my nights over the past few months. Victoria Vassar, I would like to introduce you to my Boobie. My Brian."

In Victoria's head, all that she could hear was, *To my Blue. My Blue. Damn!*

Chapter 2

"Victoria! Victoria! Someone do something." All she could hear was Rasha's panic-stricken voice. Victoria came to and thought, *What happened?* In a shaky voice, she asked, "Why am I on the floor? Why is this man now picking me up off of the floor?" *Please, Lord, this cannot be happening?*

Rasha was running around in circles. "Victoria, are you okay? Can you hear me?" Rasha was obviously concerned and had a worried look on her face. Her caring concern sounded within her voice.

Victoria was only able to whisper a faint, "Yes. W-what happened?"

Rasha said, "I knew something was wrong. She lost all the color in her face earlier and I should not have just left well enough alone and had you escorted home."

Victoria tried to assure her once again, "Rasha, I am okay. I just maybe need to eat a little something." Rasha addressed Blue, who was still holding Victoria in his arms, "Brian, take her over to the couch."

Brian Bluedell, the man Victoria has loved for the past five years of her life was now carrying her over to the couch, with this look of concern on his face as well. He was holding her in his arms, at of all places, his engagement party. "Stop looking at me that way," she mumbled under her breath. Once there, she got her wits and bearings about herself; she tried to stand to walk away so that she could get to her car as soon as possible and get out of there. When she stood, she stumbled and once again, Blue was there like lightning to help her back to her seat.

"Victoria, no!" Rasha shouted. "Stay down. That is it! You are staying here tonight. You cannot drive."

Victoria was horrified. *I would never...could never.* "Rasha, please sweetie, I am okay." She pleaded, "I promise. I will not drive. Please just call me a cab, an Uber. A Lyft." All she wanted to do was leave. *Or a spaceship? Anything?* she thought. *Just please, get me away from here.*

Rasha did not want her to be alone, but if she had to send her home, she surely was not going to do it with a stranger when she keeps passing out. "It is just past eight thirty, so I could call you a car, but no one will look out for you and your well-being that way. I would just not feel comfortable with that at all." She scanned the room and her eyes landed on Blue. "Brian will escort you. I insist," Rasha stated.

"Noooo!" Victoria shouted. Everyone except Blue looked shocked. *Oh my God. Lord, please just let me escape this moment*? She explained, "I mean; that is not necessary. Please, just call me a cab. I will be okay." She looked at Blue, who noticed a little something more in her eyes than concern.

He turned to Rasha and stated, "But babe, what about the party?"

She kissed his cheek. "Honey, this party will still be here when you get back; besides, this is more important. We got to take care of my girl."

He agreed with her, finally. "Ok, honey, if you insist."

Chapter 3

They rode in absolute silence through 24 torturous miles of breathing and the radio playing the Quiet Storm on one of Detroit's top stations. Victoria lived in Ann Arbor, a city 35 miles west of Detroit. She loved the area and the cozy, small-town feel there, so she commuted to Detroit for work five days a week. If there were late nights, the firm would put her up in a hotel for the night, so that she would not have to take the ride back so late and then have to head right back to work the next morning. This was a night that she wished she could have gotten a hotel to keep this ride from being so long. As they rode, she counted down the minutes, the miles and the seconds, just hoping that they could get through this obviously awkward experience without a hitch.

The DJ's melodic voice helped to calm her down, taking her into her own little bubble to escape this space. He took a song request from a gentleman who called in and made a request for the lady in his life. The gentleman making the request, told the story of how he knew that she was the one that he had been looking for all of his life and that he wanted to dedicate Teddy Pendergrass's, "You're My Latest, My Greatest Inspiration," to her and to let her know that he loved her. As the song played, Victoria found herself humming away to the tune. She knew it well because she has heard this song many times in her life, mostly due to the fact that Blue had sung it to her numerous times in his life. His deep baritone voice used to make her swoon. As she hummed, all of a sudden, he started singing along with Teddy P. She closed her eyes, inhaled deeply and began to absorb it all. She did not realize that she had completely once again lost herself in thought, until a single tear rolled down her right cheek. She turned to face the window for the remainder of the ride to hide her emotion. She cracked the window and let the cool September breeze brush across her face and took in three more deep breaths, with the relief of knowing that they only had five more miles to go.

Chapter 4

His head was racing with a million thoughts. *She smells the same. Everything about her still makes my skin move in ways that no one else has. I tried so hard to act as if her being there did not faze me, but when she fainted and hit that floor, all I wanted to do was pick her up and whisk her away into the night like the Dark Knight. Why was that her reaction, though? Why did she freak out when Rasha asked me to escort her home? She should know that no matter what has happened between us, that I would never let any harm come her way. Even Rasha knows that. That is why she sent me. But wait? Could it be that she still thinks about me? Man, she looked so beautiful. She looks so beautiful. Lord, what is happening?"*

Chapter 5

"Well, this is me," she said, once they pulled up in front of her condo. "Thank you for taking the time out to make sure that I got home safely. I will send for a car in the morning to bring me down to pick up my car." She was thinking, *why am I talking so much?*

He stepped out and walked around the front of the car, watching her every step of the way, until he came around and opened her door. He reached his hand out to help her out of the car. "I have to make sure that you make it in safely. Do you mind?"

She thought, *his eyes. Why, those eyes?* but responded, "I will be okay from here, I think."

He did not budge. "Your hand, please? It is my job to make sure that you make it to the door safely without losing your footing again," he chuckled. He had the greatest sense of humor and the most beautiful smile. That single dimple in his right cheek makes her love him more every time she sees it. She had to smile because she missed that about him. "Oh my God, I am so embarrassed." She covered her face and had to laugh. "What was that? I cannot believe I did that."

He looked at her and said, "But I'm glad you did."

She looked at him in bewilderment and all she could say was, "Okay. I concede."

Chapter 6

Blue helped Victoria to the door where they said their goodbyes. She sent her apologies to Rasha for ruining her party. He stated that he would not tell her that, because that was not the case. After he left, she stepped out of her clothes to take a hot shower. On the way to the bathroom, she turned on the clock radio on the nightstand. The Quiet Storm was still in play. She never felt so lost and alone. She felt so stupid and foolish. "Oh my God, Rasha." She hoped Rasha had no clue. She'd never mentioned anything about her past, especially about her love life, except for once when she told her that there was once a man that she loved deeply. Victoria had explained that she was not able to make a commitment, due to fear of it changing everything about them and everything that they were to one another. She was a person who saw her parents go from being together in unwedded bliss for 19 years and then, when they decided to get married on their 20-year anniversary, it seemed to change the relationship. They were broken apart and divorced two years later. The fear of what she saw happen to her parents has always been a thorn in her side and has always affected her romantic relationships, except when it came to Blue.

Standing there in the shower with the water trickling down her spine, the thought came through that he was a dream. He was the one man who made her feel safe. She knew that he would never do anything to hurt her and that he loved her unconditionally, but her fear of commitment made her walk away from one of the greatest things that ever happened to her in her entire life. The DJ announced the next song, "Got an online request from Jess out of Farmington Hills, who says that she and her boyfriend just broke up, and that she wants to tell him that she is sorry and to play Regina Belle's "Make It Like It Was." Then the DJ said, "Alex, this is for you. Jess says that she loves you and wants nothing more than to make it right. Playing the hits for you, right here on the Quiet Storm." Victoria started to sing along with the song as it played. She knew when she saw Blue tonight that she still loved him. In fact, she has never stopped loving him. The tears began to flow down her face like a waterfall, but the water from the shower just washed them all away. As she cried, the words came tumbling out. "What did I do? I lost the one man I every truly loved and for what? Because I was scared of what happened to my parents? Because I was scared to be loved? Because I was scared to be in love? What a fool!" The tears would not stop. It was too late. He was gone.

Chapter 7

"Why am I still here? I have a party to get back to. Rasha is going to be calling soon, wondering as to where I am, but I can't seem to pull away from this spot," Blue spoke out loud to himself. "Just go, muthafucker! Pull the fuck off! What is wrong with you? She does not want you! She left you! Left the state and all! You have this beautiful, intelligent woman who adores you and wants to spend the rest of her life with you and no one else. But, here you are, struggling with pulling away from the door of the one who left you answerless after your proposal just a few years ago! Leave! Just leave!" Blue started up the car engine and placed the gear in drive.

Chapter 8

"What are you doing? Why are you back here?" Victoria asked, sighing.

He stood there looking ever so handsome in his white cardigan and khakis and said, "I never left."

Her body began to shiver. Her mind felt weak. "Blue please, do not do this. I can't take this. Please do not do this. I beg of you, please." She never wanted to hide more in her life. He reached down, grabbed her face and placed his lips against her lips and gave her a soft gentle kiss. He looked at her eyes and could tell that she had been crying.

"You've been crying," he said, not particularly surprised. "Why have you been crying?" She put her head down and tried to hide the water once again welling up in them.

"Blue, please don't?" she whispered. She begged. She pleaded. He lifted her head and kissed her again. Her head was telling her to get out of there. Tell him to leave or simply just walk away, but she could not seem to move from that spot. She looked him in eyes and said, "Blue, please no. You have Rasha."

He looked her in her eyes and said so lovingly, "But she is not you."

Chapter 9

What this man does to me is unreal. It all feels like a dream. Blue took his time as he slowly stripped her down. He admired every curve of her body as if seeing her naked for the very first time. Kissing her neck, suckling her breasts and caressing her bottom with such a soft, gentle yet firm touch, letting her know that he has missed being next to her body as much as she has missed being next to his. He kissed her body from head to toe, starting at her forehead, then the tip of her nose and slowly slid his tongue to the outside of her lips. He lingered on her mouth kissing her into pure bliss, making her body quiver with anticipation as to what was to come next. He planted sweet kisses on her neck and chest, from the right breast and then to the left, suckling and caressing them, making her wild with more pleasure than she could ever imagine. He licked his tongue down her core, tracing her navel and then played a little game of dip the tongue within its deep cavity. Leading his way on down to "Ms. Kitty," as Victoria called her, where he lingered for what seemed like hours, giving immense intense pleasure, along with multiple orgasms. Making love to her with his tongue, stroking, flicking and sucking as if eating his last meal before his execution. She screamed, moaned, groaned, growled and howled from a place she had never seen before. And just when she felt as if she could not take any more, he entered her slowly with his massive, perfectly-shaped, perfectly-sized member and took over her body as if it belonged only to him. Their bodies meshed together as if they were one. Blue took her, in and out, in and out, over and over again, while rubbing, kissing and caressing her soft supple body. He made love to her mouth with his, giving her everything that he had in him and so much more. Their bodies intertwined, thrusting and grinding with everything that they had in them, and in unison, they both climaxed, ending a beautiful night of love and deception. Because that is exactly what it was—deception.

While still lying on top of her with their bodies still connected and breathing heavily in her ear, he whispered, "I love you and I know you still love me too. If you say the word tonight, I'll talk to her tomorrow and call off the wedding"

Victoria snapped out of her world of pure fantasy. "Wait! What? No, you cannot do that! Get off of me! Get off of me! Oh my God, Blue, what have we done?" Her mind was all scattered. "Blue, you have to go." She pushed him to the side and jumped out of the bed and started getting his things together.

He looked at her as if she was crazy. "What are you doing? Are you seriously doing this right now? What is wrong with you?"

She grabbed his shoes off the floor from just outside the bathroom door, where he left them and threw them at him, along with the rest of his clothes and once again told him, "You have to go." He climbed out of the bed and came across the room to grab a hold of her, but she dodged his grasp. "Blue, No! Leave just leave!"

He stood there. "Vicks? For real? Are you doing this right now?" The look of desperation on his face was heartbreaking.

She just needed him to go. "Blue, don't call me that, please?"

That made him smile. With a smirk on his face, he said, "It still get to you doesn't it?" He walked slowly towards her, literally backing her into a corner. She was trapped. She tried to protest, but he placed his finger on her lips as if shushing her and said, "Ok, that's it. That is all I needed to know." He gazed deeply in her eyes and stated, "You still love me."

It had started some years ago after he discovered that he had fallen in love with her. He called her Vicks, like the cream that you get out of the medicine aisle when your chest is congested. He said that she opened him up like a dose of Vick's Vapor Rub. She couldn't help but to laugh a bit. She said, "You are so freakin' corny," as she smiled at the thought. She tried to speak with such conviction, trying to mean every word that she said. "But Blue, we can't do this. This is not right. You are supposed to be at your engagement party right now. Rasha is my boss and she is becoming a very good friend to me." He looked at her as if he honestly and truly didn't even care and said nothing. She was not really surprised, because once his mind sets on something there is no changing it. She continued, "But Blue, she is your fiancée."

He grabbed her left hand, pointed to her ring finger, looked in her eyes and said, "But you were supposed to be her first." She did not know what to say. He continued, "Look, I've never stopped loving you. I've never stopped wanting you. I've never stopped needing you. You left, so that left me in a position to have to move on and by the grace of God, this situation brought you back into my life. I love Rasha, no doubt. She is a beautiful woman and she is the woman who is supposed to be my wife, but you are here and I will be damned if I do not see where this will head, before I make any rash decisions. I have never loved any woman the way that I loved you. Correction, the way that I love you. So, if you feel as if you wanna get me out of your life again, I advise for you to move back out of the state because as long as you are here, I'm coming. You hear me? I'm coming."

She shook her head in disbelief as she opened her mouth to say something, before clamping it shut, lost in his gaze. He was never more serious in his life to her than right now. He continued, "I will leave, but trust me, I will be back. You cannot get rid of me that easily. I will hold on for now, but Vicks, please know that if there is any glimpse of a chance with you, than I am taking it." He looked at her with sheer seduction in his eyes, while touching his nose to the tip of her nose and said, "And you done threw that good kitty on me too? Shiiiit! I will be back." She blushed. He stepped away, grabbed his clothes and headed to the bathroom. "Get used to it. You can't stop me," he laughed. He washed, slipped on his clothes and got ready to leave to head back to the party.

She walked Blue to the door. She was worried about Rasha wondering about his whereabouts, so she asked before he exited, "What are you going to tell her?"

He grabbed her and held her in his arms and said, "You let me worry about that. You got dropped off." He pulled her close to him while caressing her still naked bottom, entering her wet warm spot with the fingers of his free hand, while kissing her aggressively. He removed his fingers, smiled, stuck them in his mouth, removed them and said, "Til next time."

She melted, gritted her teeth and said, "Ooooo, you so nasty."

Chapter 10

Blue said out loud, "Good, got the voicemail." Blue had four missed calls from Rasha. After listening to the default message and hearing the beep, he begin to speak, "Hey Babe, sorry that I'm calling so late. Had a flat after I dropped off…Victoria, is it?" he lied. "Had to swap it out myself. I could not get road service out where I was because of the amount of time they said it would take them to get there. I am all sweaty and nasty from the tire change so when I get back, I am going to come in through the back of the house, take a quick shower and then reappear at the party all shiny and new. Love you, babe, see you soon." He hung up the phone. "That should cover me. He popped the trunk of the car. "Now to put on this doughnut."

Chapter 11

Ding Dong! Ding Dong!

Victoria was awakened by the sound of the doorbell. She glanced at the clock on the nightstand, seeing it was 6:17 am, curious as to whom in the hell would be ringing her bell that early in the morning. She was still reeling from the thought of the activities from the night before. After Blue left, she was more confused about her feelings and what was happening more than ever, so she did not get any sleep and now someone was at her door, disturbing her at this hour. She jumped out of bed, tired, irritated, hair tussled all over her head and still naked. She slipped on her house shoes and a robe and headed to the door ready to curse out the Pope himself for coming to her door at this hour. She flung open the door ready to curse and there he was, standing there with bags in hand, which was obviously breakfast.

Surprised, she said, "What are you doing here?" She was looking behind him, as if he had been followed. He just stood there with a big cheesy grin on his face.

"Evidently showing up in the nick of time," he chuckled sheepishly. "Glad it was me and not the milkman, or he would have brought your milk early every day from now on." She was confused. He gestured for her to look down and to her horror; her robe was wide open, showing off all of her glory.

"Oh my God!" She snatched him in the door. "Get in here so that I can close the door." Embarrassed yet again, all she could do was laugh a little while saying, "Blue, what are you doing here? Why are you doing this?" Blue paid her no never mind.

"Kitchen?" he asked.

She said, "Pssst, Really?" He stood there silent, patiently waiting. Realizing that he was not planning on moving until she let him know, she pointed him in the right direction. He headed to the kitchen and started searching the cabinets for plates and glassware to transfer the food from the take-out containers. Victoria looked at him and asked the same questions again. Still, he said nothing and kept on with the task at hand. "Blue, this is not going to work. This is not going to be," she said.

Blue placed fruit, the plates, and glasses on the breakfast tray that he found sitting on one of her top kitchen shelves. He then left the room and headed to the bedroom. Victoria refused to leave the spot where she was standing by the island. She didn't want no damn breakfast, she wanted answers. Blue reappeared in the kitchen, walked up to her, kissed her forehead and then reached down and swooped her up from the floor. "Blue, put me down!" she protested. He carried her to the bedroom and gently placed her on her side of the bed, which was clearly evident from the crumpled bed linen on the right side. He picked up the breakfast tray and placed it over her lap. "Okay, am I not even here? Am I talking to the walls?" she said.

He continued to ignore her and stripped down out of all of his clothes, and placed his body next to hers and proceeded to peel an orange. He broke apart a slice of the orange and fed it to her. She tried to say something to stop him, but he just shushed her thoughts away by placing the slice seductively between her lips. He repeated the act with a second slice. He then took in a slice between his lips and moved forward, placing the other end between her lips and sucked on it slowly, teasing her with the sounds, reminding her of the night before while he stared into her eyes. Blue bit off his end of the slice and rubbed it across her lips seducing her mouth, squeezing it between his lips, dripping juices on her lips, running it down her chin into the crease between her breasts. He completely engulfed the orange slice and then licked the juice from her mouth, down her chin and paid extremely close attention to her breasts.

"Blue, you have got to stop this. We need to talk about this," she said, but deep down, not really wanting him to stop. With the remaining sections of the orange, he squeezed orange juice down her neck and over her body causing it to trickle down into her wet spot giving her a burning sensation, as it ran down the middle of its folds. With juice still on his hand, he inserted his fingers in Ms. Kitty, giving Victoria a slight sting, and began to move his fingers in and out slowly mixing the orange's juice with Victoria's juices. He kissed her mouth, neck and breasts. He just kissed and kissed and kissed. "Bluuuuue, what are you doing to me?" she whispered in his ear. "Oooooh, I can't take this."

He looked her in the eyes and said, "Any and everything you want me to." He removed the breakfast tray and placed it on the floor next to the bed. Placing his head in between her legs, he licked the juice off of her that had trickled down onto her warm spot, telling her that he needed to get the remaining dose of his daily vitamin C. She laughed. She grabbed his head and spread her legs open wider, so that he would not miss out on any of the nourishment that he needed. He lapped up the mixture of juices, Victoria's and the orange's, off of Ms. Kitty like a panting dog looking for a much-needed drink. He made love to her with his tongue, licked, flicked and sucked on her clit until she began to tremble, but stopped before she released the eruption of her sexual satisfaction, wanting to look into her eyes when she climaxed. He lay down on his back and pulled Victoria on top of his body, where he helped guide her down gently on his member.

She arched her back, placed her hands on his chest and began to move slowly, taking in every bit of him, calling his name lightly. This drove him crazy. He met each stroke that she gave him with such love and affection, enforcing that he knew that she was the one and that she was always the one. When he woke up next to Rasha this morning and felt no remorse or regret from what he did the night before, he knew that it was over. He knew that the only woman he ever truly loved was right across town and he knew that he had to do everything in his power to get her back in his life. His happiness depended on it. Now, this beautiful woman that he loved so much was here with him, making love to him so passionately and so intensely that it could not be denied. She still loved him. He still loved her. He and she were meant to be one. Not him and Rasha. Victoria began to speed up the pace, sliding his member in and out of her and driving Blue mad. He grunted with each stroke she gave him and she moaned with every push back that she received. The room was filled with noises of their sexual satisfaction, letting one another know that they were both exactly where they wanted to be. In this room, in this hour, making love and pouncing upon one another like rabbits in heat.

He felt her wet spot start to contract and tighten up, pulsating on his member as she erupted for him. She wanted a breather but knew that that was not going to happen, because she knew that he needed her. He needed her so that he could succumb to his own sexual gratification of her. She relaxed her muscles and slowly let go as he lifted her body slightly, pushing his member up into her walls until she came to a place where she could begin to come down on him once again. He needed to give her what she gave him. He needed for her to know that he wanted only her, to see what she does to him. Moving at a much faster pace now, he pounded into her body, making her call out his name over and over again. She met him with such love, taking in all that he had to give her. She bounced on his member, causing their bodies to meet each other all over again, as if getting acquainted for the very first time. He blew, cursed and called her name, letting her know that she was giving him life. The more he called her name, the harder she bounced on his member, causing her bottom to shake within the palm of his hands. She braced her hands on his chest and began to move in circles, riding him to the point of him losing some of the feeling his legs. Oh, how he loved this woman. Only she could do this for him. He gripped her bottom by wrapping his arms tightly around her waist and started pounding into her, causing her to scream from the pain, but enjoy the pleasure. He pounded into her body, hard. He tried to drill a hole inside of her. He wanted to climb inside. He was trying to touch her heart with each movement he thrust up within her. Trying to push his member as far up into her as the law of physics would allow him. She cursed over and over again, trying not to pass out from the beating he was giving her, but she would not because she would miss out on all of the passion that he was giving. She knew that he was fucking her as if it were the last time. But it wasn't. It couldn't be.

She knew that she was gone. Oh how, she knew that she was gone. She shifted her body as if she was trying to run away, but Blue tightened his grip and held her down, refusing to let her move. He drove his member up and down over and over again into her as she pleaded for him to cum for her. The pace quickened. He was close to his sexual gratification. She bounced on top of him as he helped to guide her movements as she took him to ecstasy. He looked at this vision of loveliness making love to him and shouted, "I love you!" Victoria must have felt the love too, because she began to cry and said, "I know." She did not have to say it back. He knew and that was all he needed. He murmured loudly, "Oh Fuuuuck, Vicks, I'm cuuuumming."

Chapter 12

The cool night air was so refreshing. Riding on the Riverboat Cruise was one of Victoria's favorite things to do. Downtown Detroit was breathtaking at night. Smooth jazz played in the background as Victoria and Blue stood on the deck of the boat, him holding her from behind, as they took in the scenery of the city that they both loved so much. The past three weeks had been nothing short of amazing. Victoria never received more attention from Blue before than she had received within that time. Blue was there every day, attending to her needs, addressing all of her wants, granting all of her wishes and making love to her mind, body and soul. She was never happier in all of her life. Blue promised her that he would never leave her side and he was showing and proving that was his personal mission in life. Even though Victoria was still feeling like a terrible person for what they were doing to Rasha, she never wanted to be anywhere else on earth than within Blue's arms. The man she loved and the man who loved her. A gust of wind caught her off guard and caused her to shiver.

Blue held her tighter and said, "Baby, are you cold?"

She looked up at him and said, "Just a little, but I don't want to move from this spot. It's so cozy in here," meaning within his arms. He smiled.

"Well, here, take my jacket." He removed his jacket and placed it over her shoulders and wrapped her back up in his arms. They stood there just looking out onto the water bordering between the US and Canada, moving to the music, not wanting to be anywhere else in the world but where they both were at the time. Blue did not want to ruin the mood, but he knew that he needed to try to get Victoria to see the light once again. "Vicks?" he said.

She replied, "Yes darling."

"We have to tell her."

Victoria closed her eyes and swayed to the music and said, "I know, but I don't want to talk about that tonight, sweets. I just want this to be about me and you. Our moment. No work, no Rasha, just me and you, okay?"

He placed his chin gently and rested it on the top of her head and said, "Okay."

Chapter 13

"Dude what are you going to do?" Sam asked. Sam Pinkerton was Blue's best friend and silent business partner at his construction company. After Victoria left three years ago, leaving Blue confused and broken-hearted, he began to pour all of his time into his work. He met Sam through a mutual acquaintance when Blue decided to leave his former employer to become an independent contractor. After several months and several high-profile clients who praised his impeccable work and his stellar work ethic, Blue knew that he needed to make a change and needed to find an investor fast to help him in establishing his own company.

Sam was the brother of one of Blue's clients. Sam comes from a well-established family out in the Grosse Pointe Woods area, who was looking to invest in a new project. Sam was just a rich kid, who was a little bored and needed to find something to do to bide his time. He knew Blue's work and once he met him, they hit it off so well, even to the point that Blue told him from the beginning what the real reason was for him starting the company. He was honest from the start as to what made him make the move. He told him that he did not want to lie to him, that he was trying to heal a broken heart and needed something to occupy his time, and what better way to do it than to bang a hammer on some nails? Sam took a chance because he was so upfront and honest with him and it paid off, because trying to heal that broken heart is made the company extremely successful. Now, almost three years later, he and Sam are the best of friends and he is the best man for his wedding.

"Dude, only you," Sam laughed. They were playing a game of one on one on Sam's basketball court at his home and took a break to chat and catch up.

"Man, this is killing me, dog. Victoria is so determined not to say anything to Rasha, but I am ready to move on with my life. Guy, you just don't understand how much I want this to just be over with," Blue replied.

Sam shook his head, "Rasha though, man? What are you going to tell her? 'Cause she is going to be crushed. She is going to be pissed." He laughed again. "Dog, you better find yourself a bulletproof vest, because she is going to kill you. You said that she is a pretty good shot, right?"

Blue laughed along with him and said, "I know, right?" He took a swig of water. "But seriously, man, I have got to convince Vicks to do this. She says that she is happy, but I know that she is not, at least, not completely."

Sam asked, "What do you mean by that? 'She is not happy, completely?'"

Blue answered, "Well, she is so focused on Rasha that she has not given herself completely to me and our relationship, and it is starting to get to me. Don't get me wrong. I am not in a rush to hurt Rasha at all, but I am in a rush to get my life back with Victoria. The crazy part about it all though is that my fear was about her worrying about my relationship with Rasha, and what may or may not still be going on with us, but in all actuality, the real worry is not about me, but her relationship with Rasha."

Sam looked confused, saying, "Huh?"

Blue looked at Sam. "Exactly, I feel exactly the same way you do."

Chapter 14

Blue was at Rasha's, sitting on the deck next to the indoor pool, meditating. He used it to help him cleanse his aura and his thoughts when he was stressed out. The peace of just clearing his mind and just being still for five minutes a day helped to refresh him and reset his spirit. Rasha saw him through the window and called his name, "Brian."

He sighed, irritated at the fact that Rasha could clearly see that he was meditating, but she never took it seriously. He replied, "Yes."

Rasha really wanted him to come into the house when she called him but he didn't move. "Can you come here for a moment?"

Blue sighed, counted to three and then stood up reluctantly. He was deep into meditation and just wanted to be with only his thoughts. Rasha knew how focused he was during his quiet time of the day, but sometimes refused to respect it. When he arrived in the house, he headed to the kitchen where Rasha had been standing. "Yes, ma'am?"

Rasha laughed, "Yes, ma'am. Since when did I become someone's mother? Still in my prime, baby. Still in my prime." Blue gave no reaction to her joke. She saw the look of obvious irritation on his face. "Geez, what side of the bed did you wake up on today? I am sorry that I bothered you." Blue knew he was wrong and tried to apologize, but she cut him off. "I just wanted to see if you wanted to pack a picnic lunch and head out to the Children's Hospital to visit with some of the patients, and then find a little quiet spot and have a nice indoor picnic but evidently, you are having a bad day."

Blue felt terrible. Even though she interrupted his activity, he never meant to snap at her. The pressure of holding onto this lie was starting to take its toll on him and was making him unconsciously take things out on her. He apologized. "Babe, I am sorry. I have a splitting headache, so I was meditating to help to try to relieve some of the pain, so right now I am not in the best of moods." He continued, "But there was no excuse for me to snap at you that way. I was being an ass and I'm sorry," seeing that she was now clearly upset.

She said, "Yes, you were being an ass, but I accept your apology and will leave you be to finish your meditating." She walked out of the room, leaving him standing in the kitchen feeling like a pile of steaming dog shit.

"Damn!"

Chapter 15

"I can't quite put my finger on it, cuz, but something is off with this whole thing," Riley said. Riley Cassidy was Rasha's favorite cousin, who was more like her sister and also her best friend, all wrapped up into one pretty awesome individual. "The lack of intimacy, the snapping at you all the time, the nights that you cannot get ahold of him and it is always due to work? Come on, cuz." She was referring to Rasha and Blue's agreement. To avoid sleeping with Rasha and being intimate with her, Blue made the suggestion that they should abstain from physical pleasure until after the wedding. "You cannot be that naïve?" she said sarcastically. "What construction company, besides the government, do you know that is still working until one am?" She jumped up and started acting silly. "The twenty-four-hour construction guru, is still out there doing it, just for you," she joked. Rasha had to laugh because Riley was a crack-up. She was one of the funniest people that she knew.

Riley laughed and acted as if she was jokingly running a jackhammer. "Day or night? We'll get you right. Got a leak, we'll get your plumbing tight." Rasha was laughing hysterically holding her side. "Man, get the fuck out of here, Rash. Come on, cuz." They both laughed at Riley's vaudeville act, as she called it. "But seriously, cuz, you need to ask some questions here. This sounds like creepish behavior to me. I have seen Brian with you and he has always been very attentive and then all of a sudden, there is a drastic change. Something is not right and you need to find out before you make any more moves with the wedding plans." She got serious for a moment. "Look, I would never get in your business, but you know that I love you and I just don't want you to get hurt."

Rasha appreciated everything that Riley was saying, but she felt as if she knew her man. "I trust him."

Chapter 16

Blue and Victoria sat cuddled up on the couch, watching one of her most favorite movies ever, "The Miracle of Morgan's Creek." It was showing her favorite scene in the movie when Trudy Kockenlocker, played by Betty Hutton and Norval Jones, played by Eddie Bracken, were outside of her home discussing the possibility of getting a fake marriage to cover up her real marriage to a stranger, after a night out on the town with the troops, who were shipping out and just wanted one last night of fun. Victoria's laughter filled up the room. She felt that Eddie Bracken was one of the best physical comedy actors ever and laughed each and every time at something new whenever she watched the movie. Blue had never seen the movie before and was enjoying the movie, as well as enjoying Victoria watching the movie. This is what he looked forward to, Victoria introducing him to new things and new experiences. He held her tighter and she snuggled up next him even more. He could not seem to get enough of this woman. He never knew that he could be this happy. The past three years had been the longest three years of his life, but now it felt as if not one day had gone by from the way he felt about Victoria. He wanted to stay on the couch in that spot forever.

Chapter 17

Rasha had spoken to, but not seen Blue in two and a half days. She called him on this morning and told him that she wanted to spend some quality time with him tonight and that she really wanted him to make an effort to make some time for her. She let him know that she missed seeing his smile. Blue agreed to come by that evening, so she proceeded to make plans. She was beginning to feel a bit disconnected from him, so she wanted them to try to reconnect. She told Victoria earlier in the day that she was planning on leaving early, because she wanted to surprise Brian with a special night in. Rasha had a meal of lobster, crab legs, shrimp and all the trimmings ordered to the house. She ordered flowers and had them placed all around the bedroom, letting off the most aromatic flavors and essence. She stopped by Victoria's Secret and purchased a sexy black and pink teddy to seduce Brian and get him to come to the conclusion that maybe they should not wait until after the wedding, since they still have just shy of three more months to go until the big day. Besides that, she was ready and wanted to wait no longer. She wanted to make love to him and bring him back to her the way that she was used to having him. Rasha trusted Brian, but she did notice that he seemed to be losing interest in what they had together. She wanted all of him. She was not sure if maybe it was just fear talking, but she did not want to take any chances.

It was just past 8:49 and she heard Brian pulling in the driveway. She wanted to greet him in an unforgettable way, so she had already showered and slipped her cocoa butter oiled body into the teddy. Rasha was 5'7" with caramel-toned skin with a well-toned frame to match. She was an avid visitor of the gym and it showed in every muscle and curve of her body. She was particularly fond of her legs and so was Brian. He always said that he loved when she wrapped them around his body during the missionary position. That was one of his favorite things to do, he told her. She heard Blue coming through the door. She let him know that she would leave it unlocked for him. When Blue stepped in, there was Rasha damn near naked, looking damn good if he didn't say so himself, with a rose in her hair, some sexy high-heel slippers on and a smile. All he could think was, *Fuck*!

Chapter 18

After dinner, Rasha moved around the table, grabbed Blue's hand and led him to the bedroom. She told him that she knew that they agreed not to have any sex until the night of the wedding, but there was nothing wrong with a little teasing and sexual gameplay. Besides, why not be like some who claim oral sex is not really sex at all. She did not believe that, but if it got Blue's attention, she was willing to try anything. She led him over to the front of the bed, pushed him down onto it and removed his shoes. Rasha removed his shirt and directed him to lie back and just relax, "Let me take care of my big sexy baby," she said. She then proceeded to rub Blue down with some warm coconut oil that she had purchased just for the occasion. Not only did it smell nice, it was edible, in the flavor of coconut pie. Blue reluctantly laid back and wanted to get up, but his body was telling him to stay because truth be told, he was enjoying it. Blue knew that he was in trouble. He was enjoying the rub down, the massage, the attention altogether. She massaged all of his tensed up muscles, including his member. The warm oil released a very gratifying sensation and Blue felt that it felt particularly nice. She kissed his neck and licked oil off of his body. The bottom of her butt cheeks peeked from up under the teddy, showing her nice round butt cleavage. Blue found himself caressing her bottom as she massaged his member.

Before he knew it, he slipped his fingers inside, giving Rasha the type of reaction that she had been longing for. It was not what she wanted him to slip inside of her, but Rasha was in sheer heaven because she missed Blue. She missed his heavy breathing in her ear. She missed his hands on her body. She missed his kisses on her neck and chest. She missed his tongue driving her wild when he decided he wanted her for a quick little late-night snack. She knew that they both agreed to wait, but she wanted him more than ever. She whispered in his ear, "Brian, take me tonight, please? I can't handle not being with you like this." Blue knew what he was feeling was wrong, but his body was taking things into its own hands, so to speak. The more she pleaded, the more he made love to her with his hand. He truly did want to take her, but needed to remain calm, so as to not hurt Rasha's feelings or betray Victoria. Rasha met every stroke of Blue's hand, helping to guide it in and out of her warm wet spot. She looked intently into his eyes. The look on her face was telling him that she was like, *fuck the rule. I need you to make love to me*. No actually, it was saying, *dammit, I need you to fuck me*.

Blue was not sure what to do at the time, because as much as he loved Victoria and wanted to be with only her, Rasha was making it pretty hard, literally, for him not to rip the teddy off of her and take her in his arms and ravish her like a dog in heat. Rasha was a gorgeous creature and it took everything in him to try to figure out a way to leave the house before things went way too far. Way farther than what they already had. "Rasha, baby, we can't do this. We promised ourselves that we would have some type of self-control and hold off until after the wedding." He felt like a jerk for lying to her.

Rasha spread her legs wider and gyrated against Blue's hand and said, "Come on, Brian, just a little taste. Just a little hit. Just a quickie, baby." Rasha lay on her back across the bed. Blue knew that he needed to stop this before he lost all self-control, so with every stroke; he met her body faster and harder. Getting up on his knees, he watched Rasha as she closed her eyes and grabbed his wrist, lifting her hips off the bed, gyrating faster and wanting him to push his hand in deeper. Pushing his fingers in deeper, harder and faster, Blue watched her face as she slipped her free hand into her mouth and sucked on her fingers and he knew she was close to the point of no return. That was one of her signature moves when she was about to get there. Rasha gyrated and moved on his hand and climaxed, releasing a loud moan of pleasure and satisfaction. Rasha was satisfied, but wanted so much more.

She needed him to take her and she needed him to take her now. She needed to try something more. She arose and pushed Blue back down on the bed and kneeled down in front of him and tried to remove his pants. Blue knew that if she was successful at what she was trying to do, that he would not have the willpower to walk away. Blue had to find a way to get out of there now. *Think, man. Think*! Rasha began to rub his member with coconut oil, stroking it slowly and massaging it up and down. "Baby, no. We can't do this," he pleaded. Rasha paid him no attention.

"Rasha...stop, baby. Stop," he said. Rasha knew she was making him weak. Blue knew he had to do something quick. Rasha started stroking his member, while squeezing it with a firm grip at a faster pace. He was becoming more aroused with each stroke. The sound of the oil squeaking as she moved her hand up and down was driving her wild. She felt another orgasm coming on from seeing the pleasure that she was bringing to Blue. He moved his body up and down rapidly and made love within the tight grip of her palm. He cursed and moaned erotic murmurs under his breath. The mixture of her sounds and his sounds set the tone for her ultimate erotic explosion. She climaxed. Seeing Rasha once again be brought to orgasm set his body in motion for the inevitable. Blue tried not to succumb, but his gratification was met before he could stop the release. Rasha felt that she had him completely in her grasp and was going in for the kill. Blue was spent. She took advantage and moved in and licked the head of his member, licking off the ejaculation juice that flowed from the head, before coming down on it by sucking it between her lips, ready to wake it back up for another round. She licked the top of his member clean, inserted it in her mouth and pulling strongly on it with her lips closed tightly around it, but Blue intercepted her plans before she could really get started.

Blue very reluctantly wiggled his member out of the grasp of her soft juicy lips, quickly jumped up off of the bed, and grabbed his shoes and shirt from the floor. "Rasha, I have to go. We cannot do this. We agreed, so let's not throw all of our progress away," he commented. Rasha was not having it. She came at him full steam ahead because she saw that he was weak. Blue knew he had to do something drastic. He had to get the hell out of there. And fast. He did not want to, but the look on her face was telling him that he had to. "Rasha, stop!" he yelled. Rasha stopped in her tracks, stunned by his actions. "Damn, come on, man! Rasha, baby, come on! We agreed. We agreed." He didn't know what else to say. He felt like absolute shit, especially after all she had done for him that evening. He loved her. He did. But once again, he had to remind himself that he loved Victoria more. He did not want to do anything more to jeopardize what he had with her and what he was trying to build with her.

Rasha was devastated as she stood there looking dazed and confused. She turned her back to him. There was silence. From the movement of her shoulders, he knew that she was sobbing. "Rasha baby, please don't do that. I am sorry. I never meant to yell, but you wouldn't stop." He walked to her and touched her shoulder. Rasha abruptly moved away from his touch.

What have I done?

She stood with her back still towards him and asked him to leave. She stated that she just wanted to be alone. He gave one last effort to try to make it right though, before he left. "Rash, I am sorry. It is not that I don't want you because, girl, oh my God, look at you. You are stunning. Everything that a man could ask for, but baby, like I said; we agreed to hold off. I want to honor this agreement to the fullest measure. We have to trust in the process, for if we cannot trust one another in a measurement this small, what does that say about us?"

She turned and looked at him and said, "Brian, I get it, but please just leave. I just need to be alone."

Brian decided he did enough damage and turned to exit the room but before he left, he said, "Just please know that I am sorry for everything." Meaning all that he has done and all that he knew that he needed to do. He exited the house, got in his car and pulled out of the drive. Rasha lay in the empty bed and cried herself to sleep.

Chapter 19

"Dude, who is that? Damn, she's fine!" Sam asked Blue. Blue looked in the direction of where Sam was gawking and saw that he was looking in the direction of Veronica, Victoria's oldest sister and laughed.

"Dude, that is Veronica, your hostess. Vick's oldest sister." Veronica was hosting a night before Thanksgiving dinner, because she was flying to South Carolina the next day to spend Thanksgiving with her son, his wife and her grandchildren. "You mean to tell me that it's more than one of them and you been hiding this information from me?" He playfully punched Blue in the shoulder. Blue held up four fingers, indicating that there are four.

"All girls," he chuckled. Sam's eyes about popped out of his head. "They are all standing over there with her."

Sam continued his inquisition, "Married? Single? Widowed? What?" Blue had to laugh because he knew Sam and he knew Veronica, and he was not about to be any part of that time bomb that he already knew would explode. Veronica is extremely picky, and so is Sam, but nowhere near as picky as Veronica. "Naw, man…that is on you; I am out of it. You wanna know, you better walk yourself on across this room to find that all out on your own," Blue replied.

Chapter 20

Blue and Victoria sat in Veronica's oversized recliner, looking out onto the dinner party, enjoying the festivities. Blue loved Victoria's family, just like they were his own. He knew that he wanted nothing more than to make the lady in his arms always feel as if she was at home. They watched her sisters, Veronica, Vernesha, and Viola, the Vassar girls, work the room like the graceful women that they were raised to be. They were all very successful in their own rights. Veronica was a freight broker in the transportation industry, which came out to be a very lucrative business venture for her. She works from home and has five broker agents that work under her loving watchful eye, while helping to develop their skills and mindset to one day own their own business. She could also drive a semi-truck with the best of them over-the-road, so she never missed out on any opportunity to make that money, while running her six-fleet operation.

Vernesha, the second oldest, is a flight attendant but is temporarily a stay-at-home mom, married to a private pilot for one of the nation's top pop stars. She and her husband, Antonio, actually are pretty heavy in the industry of travel for private entertainment icons. Viola, the baby girl, who is always hollering that she is happily single, is a hair stylist who is in the process of opening up her dream shop that she is having built onto the back of her home with the help of her sisters, who cannot seem to sometimes see that she is the baby, but not a baby anymore. They were all the best of friends.

Even though Victoria's parents divorced after being together for 22 years, they still had the best relationship and raised their girls to be honorable women. Victoria's mom and dad were on the floor, doing a slow stride to some old school George Benson R&B tune. They clearly have never stopped loving each other. In fact, they still sneak in a date every now and then and her pops comes over for Sunday dinner at least twice a month. As the lyrics played, "I just want to hang around you. Every day and night. All of my life. Around you," Blue thought of the conversation that he and Victoria's father had earlier that evening. He told Blue that his ex-wife is the only woman he ever loved and will ever love and if he could do it all over again, he wouldn't change a thing about his life with her because it was good. He also told him that he was glad to see him step up to move forward to get Victoria back into his life, because he always liked him and knew that he also was good for his daughter. Blue appreciated the blessing from her father, not once, but twice, so he knew that he wanted nothing more than to make him proud. He looked around Veronica's great room and saw so many loving scenes. Vernesha and her husband were playing with the baby on the floor in the corner. Next to them, Viola, along with her best friend, Luciano, who she has known since they were seven and who attended most of their family events, were now sitting cross-legged with her niece and nephew, playing a game of jacks and getting beat, from what he could tell, pretty badly at the game. He watched Sam as he talked Veronica's ear off in a corner of the room. She seemed to be enjoying his conversation because she was laughing up a storm. He thought, *Boy, is Sam in heaven. That is his weakness. A woman laughing at his corny ass jokes*. He chuckled. Victoria moved closer and wrapped his arms around her more. She always told him that this was her favorite place to be; it was his as well, his favorite place for her to be. He kissed her on her cheek and whispered in her ear that he loved her. He smiled and thought, *this is the life. This is my life. This is exactly where I want to be.*

Chapter 21

Three weeks had gone by since the incident at Rasha's place. Rasha and Blue were in a better place, emotionally, since that night. She had started talking about the wedding plans more with Blue because the date was approaching fast. Rasha continued to work her normal hours, but it seemed as if she spoke of Blue a little less than usual, Victoria noticed. Rasha never told Victoria about that night because she was embarrassed by his actions. Blue only mentioned that they had dinner because he showed up at Victoria's house that night and made passionate love to her like his life depended on it. He tried to convince her once again to tell Rasha and yet again, she would not bite. She was okay with things for now. She did not want to ruffle any feathers, as Blue called it. She loved her job and what it did for her confidence and her career. She was becoming one of the top consultants at the firm, even with the short amount of time that she had been there. She just wanted everyone to be happy. She was happy. Or was she really? All she knew is that she did not want to start any trouble. Things were just going too good.

 But truth be told, it was really starting to get to her and she was in the worst mood, trying to fight off this apparent sickness that seemed as if it wanted to take over her body. She just knew it had come about after being on the jazz cruise in the cold night air, but she did not care because she was with the man she loved. She did not care but she sure was starting to regret it, because she felt horrible today.

Chapter 22

Later that day, just before lunch. "The décor for the wedding will be a Winter Wonderland theme," Rasha bragged to Victoria. "We are even going to go to Colorado to ski for our honeymoon to keep with the theme." Victoria was so sick of hearing about the wedding, but there was really nothing that she could do about it. She was irritated by any and everything that Rasha said today for some reason. She and Blue were trying to figure some things out and it was so hard, because of the situation with Rasha.

She just wanted this conversation to be over with, so she tried to change the subject. "The Alexander account is coming along pretty nicely, don't you think?" she interrupted.

Rasha thought it was a little rude but replied, "Yes, they all seem to be pretty happy with the results. We should be able to present the numbers by week's end, letting them know where we stand and how much they will be able to profit within the next three quarters. Mr. Alexander, the president, has given great praise for all that you have done in making this a success. I am very proud of the work that you have done also."

Victoria accepted the compliment and said, "Well, thank you for entrusting something of this magnitude within my care. I really appreciate the chance to be able to help with this project."

Rasha said, "Victoria, there is no thanks necessary. You are great at what you do. Hell, you make me look good. Glad I had the good sense not to let you get away." Rasha was texting someone on her phone. "Geez, I am starving. Texting Brian to see if he will bring me some lunch. There is a little bistro near his current job site that sells a pastrami club sandwich that's to die for. Oh, and some broccoli cheese soup will go great with that."

Victoria just wanted her to stop talking. *She always finds her way back to bring up Blue.*

"Before I hit send, would you like anything?" she asked.

Victoria nodded her head no but said under her breath, "Yeah, I wish you would shut the hell up."

Chapter 23

The last few months have been crazy. Blue and Victoria have been so hot and heavy, but the guilt of lying to Rasha was starting to taking its toll on her. On top of that, Blue kept insisting that they tell her, because he no longer wants to live a lie. He wanted to respect Victoria's wishes, but wanted to show Rasha respect as well by not deceiving her anymore. He was tired of feeling as if their love was a secret, also. He stated, "Vicks, it is not that we don't both love her, but we love one another more, so we deserve to be happy and as long as this secret goes on, none of us will ever get to that place."

Victoria feels as if Rasha has entrusted her with the business and for her to just stab her in the back is not something that she wants to do, even though she is really already doing it. Coming to work and having to look this woman in her face daily, listening to her gushing and cooing about the man that she is so in love with, who happens to be the same man that Victoria's is in love with, was starting to make her sick. Literally. She had been nauseous and sick for what seemed like weeks now.

"Victoria, you are still not feeling well?" Rasha asked while they were going over the books of the Alexander account.

"Not really. I must have some type of bug. I just can't seem to shake this. I think that I am going to go ahead and go to the doctor this afternoon after work. See if they can give me something to settle my stomach or at least let me know what this is."

Rasha agreed, "Yes, that would be wise. Matter of fact after we wrap things up here, go ahead and cut out early for the day. Go get yourself checked up."

Victoria asked, "Are you sure? I can bear this until this afternoon, besides we have that conference call later for the Barksdale, Hayes & Thornton account."

Rasha responded, "Yes, go ahead. I can handle the conference call solo this afternoon. They are just calling to check up on the progress that has been made so far. You will have plenty of time to meet with them later." Victoria agreed to take her up on the offer and thanked her. Rasha continued, "I swear if I didn't know better," she laughed, "I would swear that you were having a baby, but I know better than that because you are not seeing anyone."

Victoria laughed along with her nervously. "Yeah, I know right."

Heading to the doctor's office she thought that it could not be possible. Granted, yes she had not seen her period in a while, but she just chalked it up to the stress of the secret. Besides, she and Blue always used protection; plus she is on the pill. She was listening to a male enhancement commercial on the radio when all of a sudden, like being struck by lightning, it hit her. *Oh my God, Oh my God, Oh my God, Nooooo,* she thought. *The morning he showed up with breakfast.* She said out loud, "There was no protection!"

Chapter 24

"How far along are you, sis?" Veronica asked. After leaving the doctor's office, Veronica was the first person that she called. Vernesha and Viola were already over at her house, so she placed the call on speaker.

"Doc says about twelve weeks." She felt so ashamed.

They all said in unison, "Twelve weeks!" Victoria felt so small.

Vernesha said, "What are you going to do? Have you told Blue yet?"

Victoria answered, "No and I don't know if I am going to right away. He is already on my head about letting Rasha know and if I mention the baby, he will tell her for sure, with or without me." Victoria began to cry. "All he wants to do is be with me and be happy and he has always wanted a family and this is so unfair that it has to come about like this. I should have never come back here. I am so ashamed."

Veronica was getting angry. She cut her off and proceeded to chastise Victoria for that comment. "Vicky, now you know that is some bullshit. What the hell do you have to be ashamed of? A man loving you? A man wanting to be with you? A man wanting to be there and take care of you? I feel for Rasha, I do, but the truth of the matter is that you and Blue are destiny and no one can change that."

Viola was pacing the floor and was getting angrier by the second at Victoria. Viola jumped in, "Blue is right. You should not have let this go on this long. You should have both told her the night of the party. Now, almost three plus months have gone by, and now you sit here twelve weeks pregnant, by the man that you love and you are over there feeling guilty, instead of calling the love of your life and enjoying this moment. Girl, bye! You better get the hell over it, grow the fuck up and get this together, sister! You brought this all on yourself!"

Vernesha tried to cut her off, "Viola!"

Viola shouted, "No, Nesha, she needs to hear this!" Veronica gestured to Vernesha to stop and just let Viola talk. "Left that man to fend for himself for years. For three damn years! And now he is back, trying to give you the life you had and even more and you over there acting like this is the end of the world. Man, if only half of us single women could find a man that loves one of us just half as much as he loves you, we would be in heaven. Ugh! Let me shut the hell up! Man, this fool is trippin'!" Viola walked out of the room, mumbling expletives.

Vernesha said, "Don't pay her attitude no mind, but you know that she is right, sis."

Veronica agreed and said, "You did this, so suck it up. Grow the hell up, as La La said and go be happy in your life, with the one that you were meant to be with. Now, I am sorry, sis, we love you and would never do anything to hurt you or make you feel less than, but you needed to hear that." Victoria knew they were right. She was the one who left him answerless, then ran away. She was the one who did not insist that he leave that morning. She was the one who did not insist that he not take her home on that faithful night, which led to that next morning. Blue wanted to tell her weeks, months ago but she kept begging him not to; she was the one who let this go on this long. What has she gotten herself into? All she could say was, "At this point, we have to tell her."

Chapter 25

Blue and Rasha were heading out to dinner for Japanese cuisine. Rasha was speaking to him about her day at work, but he was not really listening as he was lost in his thoughts. He had not heard from Victoria in two days. She was not returning his texts or answering his calls. He was so busy with a project on the site that he did not have time to run out to Ann Arbor for a pop-up visit, to find out what the hell was going on. He had already decided that he was going to find out on today, but he'd promised Rasha last week that they would make a dinner date for Thursday night and it was now Thursday night. Rasha tried to convince him otherwise in the beginning about the physical pleasure issue, but was beginning to enjoy the perks of no intimacy besides a little rubbing and kissing, because he seemed to become more attentive in other ways.

He was thinking about Victoria when he heard Rasha mention her name. "Wait? What did you just say?" he asked her. He wanted her to repeat what she had just said. Rasha looked at him a little strange, but repeated the comment. "I was just saying that I had not heard from Victoria in a couple of days and I wanted to check in on her, but she is not answering my calls." He tried to pry without it seeming too obvious to see if she maybe knew some more information. "You think everything is alright?" She was scrolling through her phone, looking for Victoria's personal email so that she could send her a message. "Well, she had not been feeling well for a couple of days, so I suggested that she go to the doctor on Tuesday. She went after leaving work early and then called off the rest of the week. Said that she was alright, but it was suggested to her that she just needed to rest and stay out, in case she was contagious."

Why did she not tell me that she was sick? I would have come to take care of her. She knows that. He smiled slightly at the thought. *But that is why she did not tell me, because she knows that I would come take care of her. That is her problem. Always thinking about every damn body else and not herself. But that is why I love her. She is like no other.*

Rasha continued laughing, "She has been sick and nauseous for about three weeks now and I made a joke that, if I did not know better, I would swear that she was pregnant, but I know that she is not seeing anyone." Blue was startled, swerving, he hit the rumble strip on the side of the expressway and then hastily snatched the car back onto the lane.

Rasha gasped, "What the hell? Are you alright!"

He had to think fast. "Swerved to miss a box on the road."

A box? Really? Dummy! he thought.

She did not see any box, but then again, she was looking down at her phone at the time.

"Well, what are you going to do? You have no other way to get in touch with her?" She looked at him. He continued, "I mean, I know that she is someone that you care about, so there is no one else that you can call to make sure that everything in alright?"

Still looking at him, but now with the side eye, she said, "No one," while thinking to herself, *what the fuck was that?*

Chapter 26

Blue was completely unable to focus and Rasha noticed it all throughout the dinner. She did not want to seem as if she did not trust him, but he was distant and distracted by something. *Or someone?* She wanted to believe in him with everything that there was within her, but he was sure making it hard for her to do so.

Rasha thought that something was happening and she was not sure what it was, but she made it her vow to sure as hell find out.

Mr. Brian Bluedell, what are you up to?

Chapter 27

Once they were finished with dinner, Blue took Rasha home. Since they'd decided to not share in the act of physical pleasures, they made the mutual decision that it was best that they not spend the night with one another, in order to avoid temptation. Rasha completely trusted him, so she had no issues with this arrangement, but for some reason this night he seemed to be in a rush. Blue acted as if he didn't even want to walk her to the door. His mind was racing and all he could think about was hitting the freeway and going west to find out what was wrong with Victoria. "Are you not coming up for a while, Boobie?" He kissed her on the cheek and told her that he was tired and had a long day, and just needed to get some rest. "Besides, you look too good tonight, baby. I might break some rules and we both don't want that." She felt funny about what was going on, but she went ahead and agreed reluctantly and allowed him to walk her into the house and then head on out the door. As he pulled off, she stood in her picture window and watched his car until the rear lights disappeared.

Chapter 28

Boom! *Boom*! *Boom*! *Ding Dong*! *Ding Dong*! She already knew who it was before she got to the door. Victoria swung open the door and instantly turned around to walk back to the bedroom. She had been sleeping. Seems as if that was all she did for the past two days, was cry and sleep. "You did not have to try to knock the door down. A regular bell ring would have been sufficed," she said sarcastically. "Lock the door behind you please. And before you start, I am sick and I am not in the mood to be jumped on like a jack rabbit tonight, so if that is why you are here, you can just jump right back in that pretty little black car of yours and take it on back to the D."

He was furious. No communication for two days straight and then he comes in the house to an attitude, after he rushed out to make sure that she was alright. She had on some little pink boy leg cut pajama shorts and a royal blue tank top and her fuzzy house socks. He had noticed it a little before but it was more than clear that she had gained a little weight in her butt and in her thighs, but it never dawned on him before. "When were you going to tell me?" Victoria kept walking as if she did not hear him. He repeated, "When were you going to tell me?"

She stopped, turned and looked at him as if she was irritated by the sound of his voice and the look on his face. "Tell you what?" she asked.

Blue tried to stay calm. "That you are pregnant."

She turned around and went into the bedroom and said, "Well, evidently, somebody has been running their mouth at your house."

He was pissed, absolutely livid. "My house? What the fu...? You ignore me for two fucking days straight, with no explanation, no warning and you got the nerve to be mad because Rasha mentioned to me that you were sick and that you went to the doctor? She does not know that you are pregnant. She just thinks that you are sick, which evidently you are, but in the head!" Angrily, he began to pace the floor. "When she mentioned about the joke of you being pregnant, I came up with that conclusion. So you leave her out of this!"

Victoria stepped back out the room. "Oh, so we defending the bitch now?" she yelled. "We gone come in my house and check me about another woman? Dude, now I know you done lost your damn mind!" She crossed her arms and tapped her foot rapidly, waiting for his response. All he could do was laugh angrily.

"Your ass is crazy! What the fuck am I doing? Oh my God! Are we really doing this right now? This is supposed to be one of the happiest moments of my life, me finding out that I am going to be a father. Having my seed, with the woman of my dreams and this is how you act? You cheat me out of my experience of trying to love you unconditionally not once, but twice and then this? I don't get the courtesy of knowing this important information and then you try to check me at the same time about my relationship with Rasha, that you clearly care about more than the relationship that you have with me."

Victoria knew she was wrong, but it did not stop her. "Look, I told you that I did not want to do this. I did not want to like you. I did not want to love you. I did not want to trust you. I just did not. I did not. But you were so determined to keep coming at me. I asked you to go. I asked you to leave me alone. But you didn't." Victoria broke down into tears. "But you made me. Blue, you made me love you. Blue, I love you so much, but I can't handle this. This deception is killing me. I can't be this happy, knowing that I am going to destroy someone in the process. This is so unfair. This is so freaking unfair."

Blue was still furious, but seeing her cry softened his mood. He held open his arms. "Baby, come here." She walked into his arms and fell against his chest. He rubbed her head, as she sobbed into his chest, and spoke softly in her ear, "Baby, we are in this together, but that is the key word. Together." He lifted up her chin, so that he could look into her eyes. Her eyes were closed. "Baby, look at me." She looked into his face and could see all the love he had inside of him, that was meant just for her. "You have got to stop fighting us and start fighting for us. I need you to know that I am going nowhere, so stop trying to push me away because the harder you push me, the harder I am going to push back to get to you. You don't find a love like this and throw it all away. And Vicks, now you are having my baby? You must be crazy, if you think that I am going anywhere." She smiled. "God saw fit to bring us back here after separating us for three years. Three years, baby! We missed out on three years. I am not willing to miss out on three more days. I am done with this." He looked her in her eyes and said, "Marry me? Tonight."

Chapter 29

"Damn, I lost him. Why is he in Ann Arbor? What the hell is going on out here?" Rasha mumbled. "Damn, Victoria, where are you when I need you? This is your neck of the woods. This is the time I need you to be my friend, for real. But that is okay, I am going to ride up and down every single one of these streets until I find your ass, Brian, if it takes me all night." She rode through the streets, scanning her surroundings, looking for Blue's car. "Where did you go?"

Chapter 30

Blue and Victoria pulled up to Rasha's house, but her car was not there. Victoria was relieved but she knew that they had to tell her and that they had to do it tonight. They were headed to Vegas to get married right after. She knew that she would probably lose her job, but Blue was right. She had to fight for her family. They were now officially a family and there was no going back now. A baby would be here in just six more months.

Chapter 31

Rasha sat down the street from her house and watched as his car pulled in her drive. She cut off the lights and waited to see what their next move was. "Who the hell is that in the car with him?" she spoke "and why would he bring them to my house this time of night?"

Back in Ann Arbor, Rasha was about to give up the search, when she decided to go back to the freeway entrance heading back in the direction of Detroit and waited to see if she would spot his car. After about 35 minutes, he entered the ramp, but had a passenger in the vehicle. Her first thought was, *this muthafucka has the nerve to come pick up someone to take them back to his house. This is why he wanted no intimacy, so he can sneak women to his house*? She gave him a few feet and then followed him, staying at least two car lengths behind. She was thrown when he did not come off at his exit, but continued on down the expressway for seven more miles and came off at the exit leading towards her home. And then was even more shocked when he turned on her street and pulled into her driveway.

Chapter 32

After sitting in Rasha's driveway for about 30 minutes, Blue decided to go ahead and leave. This would have to wait. He never wanted to hurt Rasha and neither did Victoria, but he was not in a position of wanting to wait any longer to finally make this lovely lady sitting next to him his wife. As they were backing out of the drive, Rasha pulled up behind them. Victoria got a lump in her throat. Blue was holding her hand and he felt her whole body tense up. He looked at her and said, "It's okay, baby. We can do this. We have each other and that is all that matters."

She said, "I know. I love you."

He gave her hand a squeeze, saying, "I love you too." They exited the car.

Chapter 33

"Victoria?" Rasha was surprised to see her. She was so relieved. Here she was running around, following this man and him with his sweet self, went out to go make sure that Victoria was alright for her, because he knew that she was so worried. "Girl, where have you been? I was so worried." She hugged Victoria. She looked at Blue and said, "Baaaby, you are so sweet. You knew this and you went out and checked up on her for me? Am I the luckiest girl in the world or what?" She leaned in to kiss him on the lips and he stepped back. It was one thing to keep up the charade, but in no way was he going to let her kiss him with Victoria present.

Rasha stepped back and said, "What was that?" she laughed. "Since when did you become so shy?"

Blue looked at Victoria and then to Rasha, and said, "We need to talk."

Chapter 34

"Rasha, please understand!" Victoria pleaded but Rasha was not hearing it.

"Get out! Get out! Get out!" After Blue stated that they needed to talk, Rasha was concerned and became worried. She knew that this had to be serious, so she invited them into the house. They both said that they thought that it would be best to talk outside, but Rasha insisted that she would never put her business in the streets and went into the house. She left the door open for them to follow behind. Once in the living room area, Blue went on to explain that he had made a mistake by leading her on, knowing that he was still in love with another woman from his past, and that they had reconnected. He went on to say that he knew that he loved her more than ever now.

Rasha was hurt and embarrassed. She felt as if she was tricked. Bamboozled. "So, this is why you went to go get Victoria, to comfort me in my time of pain? To embarrass me in front of my friend like this? How dare you? Why would you do that to me?" Rasha began to cry and just wanted him out of her sight. She continued, "You tell me that there is another woman from your past. Where the hell was she when you needed her in your time of need? Where was she when your mother died?" That hit Victoria to her heart's core. She loved his mother and she was not around for him when she passed. "Where was she when your company was about to fold and you needed a shoulder to cry on? Where was she when you were sick and laid upstairs in my bed for four days back-to-back, when I nursed you back to health? Where was she then?"

Victoria felt terrible. She watched Rasha as she ranted on about how hurt she was. "Rasha, please understand," Victoria said, before realizing that she said it.

Rasha stopped, stepped back and began to read her body language. She looked at Victoria. "Wait?" Rasha looked at her and then back to Blue. She took it all in and began to think back. "The party? Your face all flushed? The daydreaming? You fainting when I introduced you two?" She looked at Blue. "The distance? The attitude? The sudden need to not be intimate anymore?" She was flabbergasted. She turned back to Victoria and said, "It's you?"

Victoria tried to explain but the words would not come out.

Blue tried to step in, but Rasha continued, "Oh my God! The flat tire! That is why you were late getting back to the party. You were with her, weren't you?" Blue felt like such a heel for hurting this woman he cared about so deeply and actually did love; it was just that he loved Victoria more. She was the love of his life. His one true love. Rasha rested her hands on top of her head as if she had a splitting headache. "You would not make love to me that night, because you had already made love to her, didn't you?" Blue was silent. She looked back at Victoria, "And you? You sat up and pretended to be my friend?" Victoria was crying and trying so hard to make everything alright, but there was nothing that could make that a reality. Rasha wanted to crawl into a hole and die. She stood in the middle of her living room floor, with her heart breaking from not only the man that she was supposed to marry, but also from the woman who was supposed to be her friend. This led her back to Victoria missing in action, since going to the doctor on Monday afternoon. She looked at Victoria, tears in both of their eyes and asked the question that she did not want to know the answer to. "Victoria? You're having Brian's baby, aren't you?"

Victoria felt as if she was crying a thousand tears. "Rasha, I'm so sorry." Rasha fell back onto her sofa, wanting nothing more than to run away from this place. "I never meant to hurt you. If I would have known that it was Blue that you were engaged to—"

"Blue?" Rasha cut her off. She looked back and forth at them both, gave a chuckle, a smirk with a sinister smile and shook her head. She looked at Blue and rolled her eyes.

Victoria looked at Blue and thought maybe they should leave but she continued, "I would have never come to the party. I would have never come to the firm."

Rasha laughed a vicious laugh and said, "You got that right. Bitch, you're fired!"

Blue stepped in, "Now wait a minute, Rasha, this has nothing to do with her job or her work performance."

Rasha looked at Blue with the evil of seven demons. "You think I would let this whore back in my firm , where I would have to sit up and look at this sad face bitch every day? You got to be stupider than you look right now!"

Blue stepped towards Rasha and Victoria stopped him. "Now look here, Rasha, she is no one's whore and definitely no one's bitch," he seethed.

Rasha kept laughing. "Oh, hit a nerve did I?"

Blue continued angrily, "She was the one who wanted to move past this to avoid hurting you. She was willing to sacrifice her happiness for your happiness, but I would not have been happy without her, so don't you dare try to put this on her. Don't you dare attack her. This is all on me."

This is what led to them being told, "Get out; get out of my home, at once."

Blue said, "Vicks, let's go. You do not need this stress in your condition." Since she'd decided to attack Victoria, the gloves were off so he wanted to give Rasha one last sting by looking her in the face and saying, "Besides, we have a wedding to get to."

Chapter 35

The sound of the ambulance could be heard in the distance. They had just made it past the Indiana state line on I-94 West when they were hit from the side and pushed into the embankment, causing the vehicle to spin out of control, flip once and land back on all four tires. Blue was stunned and knocked semi-unconscious, but somehow quickly recovered when he saw Victoria lying motionless in her seat. "No, no, no no, no, no, no. Baby, get up. Baby, get up!" He tried to awaken her, but got no response. He managed to get out of the car and get her out of her seatbelt, and pull her from the wreckage. She had a giant gash on the side of her forehead from it hitting the passenger side window during impact. She was bleeding from her midsection, but he did not know from where. He sat her down on his lap on the ground and tried to wake her again. A crowd had now formed on the side of the expressway where Victoria lay unconscious in Blue's arms.

"Baby! Baby! Vicks, baby, wake up! Please wake up! Help! Someone help, please!" He looked around helpless, not knowing what to do. "Baby, please wake up." Blue was hysterical. "Someone help her, please! Someone, please get some help!" Blue held Victoria in his arms and rocked her back and forth, while tears ran down his face from the fear of losing her. "God, please don't do this. Please, God? I need her. God, please don't do this." Blue sat with Victoria in his arms, unsure of what had happened. He was bleeding from a cut on his arm and his side hurt, possibly from some broken ribs, but he did not care or even feel any real pain because he could only focus on Victoria. "God, please don't do this to my family. This is my family. God please, please don't do this." He could hear a woman's voice in the distance screaming that she was sorry and that she did not mean to do it. Whoever it was, was being restrained by two men who saw what happened and wanted to make sure that she did not get away with what she had done.

At the same time, the ambulance was pulling up. Blue stood up with Victoria in his arms and ran to the ambulance before they were even able to stop the vehicle. "Please help her, please!" The paramedics quickly helped Blue place Victoria on the gurney. "She is twelve weeks pregnant, my fiancée, the mother of my child and the breath that I breathe. Please do not let me lose her." The paramedic felt for this man who obviously loved this woman. "Sir, we can only promise that we will do our best."

Chapter 36

A fire burned within her stomach that sent her into an absolute rage. "Bitch, you think that you get to have my man after your stupid ass gave him up?" She laughed, "Ha! A wedding? Not in this lifetime!" After Blue and Victoria exited from her home, she took off after them without their knowledge.

Chapter 37

It was said that she just could not take it. Rasha knew that she was going back to jail after she was released on bond. The judge denied her for the first six weeks due to the nature of the crime and the amount of people that witnessed the event. She not only hit Blue's vehicle, but caused two more accidents in the process of chasing Blue's car down. No one ever thought that she would go that far.

Victoria fell into a deep state of depression after everything happened. Upon waking up at the hospital, wondering where she was and what happened, Blue also had to tell her that there was a possibility that the baby would not make it, but as of now, that it was just too early to tell. She had to stay on constant bed rest for the next three weeks to make sure that everything would be okay with the baby, due to some broken ribs and a deep laceration on her abdomen and her lower back.

As Blue stood there looking at the woman that he hurt so badly, he wished that he could do it all over again and would have told her that first night he saw Victoria. The night he knew that nothing was going to keep him from her. He did love Rasha. She was a good woman to him. He cared for her deeply, but to stand here and see her lying here in a casket, hit home. Word is that after she was bonded out, she took care of some affairs, including sending a note to Blue, apologizing for everything that she had done, actually saying that she understood that when true love finds you, that no matter how much you try to run away from it, it will always track you down.

Brian,

I know that I am the last person that you ever thought you would hear from, but I needed to get some things off of my chest. First off, I would like to say that I forgive you. I know that that sounds strange coming from me, after what I did to you and your family. Your family? That still gets to me, but I know that you were never out to hurt me intentionally. I know that Victoria was the true love of your life. I have always known that our connection was never really one for the books, but I was happy that you loved me and cared for me the way that you did, and I knew that my love would pull us through whatever would have the gumption or the audacity to come our way. Everything that is, except Victoria. I knew that there was a love that left you empty on the inside, but all I wanted to do was try to fill that void. A lot of us think that we have that power, but no one does, not when it comes to true love. When true love finds you, no matter how much you try to run away from it, it will always track you down. I can't be mad because it found you. You deserve every bit of happiness in your life and I mean that from the bottom of my heart. The second thing I would like to say is that I hope that one of these days, you can forgive me. There is no excuse that can ever justify my actions. I was lost in a place that I have never seen before and I am so sorry. I am sorry that I hurt Victoria. I am so sorry that I hurt your family, but most of all, I am so sorry that I hurt you. You were and will always be my one and only true love. Goodbye.

Loving You Until the Day I Die,

Rasha Du`Voe

Sometime after sending that letter, she decided to take her own life. In her suicide note, it was said that she could not live out her days locked up as a prisoner, due to being charged with three counts of attempted manslaughter, aggravated assault and endangering the lives of others.

He never meant for any of this to happen. All he could do was say, "I'm sorry and I forgive you, Rasha," and then walk away. He never told Victoria about the note.

Chapter 38

"Do you, Brian Marquis Bluedell, take Victoria Moniecia Vassar, as your lawfully wedded wife to have and to hold from this day forward, for better or for worse, for richer or for poorer, in sickness and in health, until death do you part?" the priest asked.

"I do," he answered. And do you Victoria Moniecia take Brian Marquis….. "I do."

The priest turned and addressed the wedding party, "At this time, the bride would like to say a few words to her husband to be." Blue was unaware of this and was curious as to what was about to happen. Victoria looked to the organist, bass player and drummer, who started to play Teddy P's, "You're My Latest, My Greatest Inspiration." Blue looked at her in awe and suddenly lowered his head.

As the music played, the organist started singing the lyrics to the song softly. "I've been so many places, I've seen so many things, but none quite so lovely as you."

Victoria lifted his head to see tears welling up in his eyes. She placed her right hand on his left cheek and mouthed the words, "I love you."

The organist continued, "More beautiful than the Mona Lisa, worth more than gold, and my eyes have the pleasure to behold."

As the music played, she looked into his eyes with all of the love that she had in her for him and said, "There are not enough words on this earth to express how I feel about you, but I am going to try with the limited amount that there is in the English vocabulary, to let you know what you are to me. I don't know what I did to deserve someone so loving and amazing as you. You loved me even when I didn't love myself. I fought you every step of the way, because I thought that there was no way that I deserved someone this phenomenal to be in my life, but you refused to give up on me. You once told me that I have got to stop fighting us and start fighting for us, and that you were not going anywhere, so to stop trying to push you away because the harder I pushed, the harder you were going to push back to get to me. Baby, thank you for the push back. Thank you for pushing back with a force that only God saw fit for you to be able to do. Your words, you don't find a love like this and throw it away. You are my life. My love. You are the cocoon that changed me from a caterpillar to a butterfly. You are my happiness, my joy, my elation, my high and sometimes even my headache."

The entire church laughed. She continued, "But I would gladly walk around with it for the rest of my life, taking no pain medication as long as I know that it was all because of you. It is said that we all are put here to make someone's life better. You, my love, are what God put on this earth to make my life and me better. With only the help of God, baby, you are, my greatest inspiration."

Chapter 39

She lay in the hospital bed in labor, pushing out the final piece of the puzzle to now make her family whole. Dr. Berry said, "Okay Victoria, when you feel your next contraction, I want you to push. One last push and you can finally meet this lovely little individual of yours that is ready to take over your world." Victoria was so tired. Blue was there by her side, holding her head and wiping the sweat from her brow. "Okay, let me know when you feel your next contraction," Doc continued.

Blue saw that by the look on Victoria's face, she was ready. "Doc, it's coming!" she shouted.

Blue held her hand tightly. "Okay, baby, you can do it. Push, baby." Victoria gave one last good push and he was here. Their son was here. Blue could not be prouder. He was someone's dad. "Oh my God, baby. You did it. Look at him. Look at my boy!" he beamed.

Victoria looked at him tiredly, but was so in love at first sight. Her son was here. Brian Marquis Bluedell, Jr was seven pounds, three ounces of pure beauty. She had never been happier in her life. As she looked at her family, she couldn't help but think that sometimes, just jumping and taking a chance is the best decision that can be made."

Blue looked at her and could tell she was deep in thought. He asked, "Vicks, what's on your mind?"

She looked at him and simply said, "We're so blessed."

He smiled, kissed her on her forehead and said, "I know."

Chapter 40

"Bring him here," Veronica insisted. "Bring me my new nephew." Victoria and Blue had arrived home to a house full of family and friends waiting to meet the baby. All of Victoria's sisters were there, her parents, his siblings, Luciano, Sam and a host of family and friends. Brian Jr. came home to a loving environment of cooing aunties, cousins and friends. Blue loved it.

Sam approached him with a cigar. Even though neither Blue nor Sam smoked, he just thought it appropriate for the occasion. "Congratulations, man!" Sam said. "Old man is now a pops. Man, I could not be prouder of you, dude." He gave Blue a shoulder to shoulder bump of brotherly love.

"Man, I did not think I could ever be this happy. This is crazy that this is my life," Blue said.

Sam looked at him and couldn't help but to envy what he had with Victoria. "I am so happy for you, man. You deserve it, dude. You are good people and I want to see nothing but good things come your way."

Blue thanked him for the kind gesture and responded, "Thanks. But what about you, man? You need to find your queen out here in the world too." Sam looked across the room and spotted Veronica, who was loving on the baby and said, "I'm working on it, man. I'm working on it."

Lette

Lette

V is for Veronica

A Day in the Life of Them Vassar Girls Series Novel
Book II / Volume II

V is for Veronica

A DAY IN THE LIFE OF THEM VASSAR GIRLS

SERIES NOVEL

Lette

BOOK II / VOLUME II

Dedication/Acknowledgement

January 8, 2017

My Loves,

Once again I come to you, Lord, thanking you for the blessings that you have bestowed upon me. Thank you for the vision and the lessons in life to be able to put this one on paper. Thank you for letting me be one who believes in true love. Thank you for letting me know that no matter what happens in life that it will all work out in the end. Thank you for the loves I have had and the loves that I have lost. Thank you, Lord, for never letting me settle for anything less than what is meant for me. Thank you for the power of goodbye and then thank you also for the power of hello. Hello, world. This is a craft that has become an instrumental part of my world. It is therapy at its finest being able to share with you all, what fantasies develop within my big ole head. When I started the first book in this series, that was not really what it was intended to be. As I wrote, V is for Victoria (which was not the original title) and tried to explore the relationship between Victoria and her sisters, it came to me that I felt compelled to go a little further into her sisters' lives as well and thus *A Day in the Life of Them Vassar Girls* was born. A novel series, focused on a love story that makes you feel at home in your life of love. So after I typed the last letter on the page ending Victoria's story, I immediately opened up a new blank document and wrote the first 4 chapters of Veronica's story before laying my head to sleep that night and by night two, I was up to chapter 18 and less than a week later, it was complete. These characters have started to become near and dear to my heart, immediately feeling like family, because they are all of part of me in some way. Thank you for allowing me to share a part of me through my extended family with you.

xoxo xoxo

Love,

Lette

Chapter 1

gracious hostess to her guests, working the room and having so much fun at the dinner party that she was throwing for the family for the holiday. She was heading out on Thanksgiving Day on an early morning flight to spend it with her son, his wife, and her 2 grandchildren in South Carolina. Since this was her year to host Thanksgiving, she decided to do a night before Thanksgiving dinner so that she could keep up her end of the bargain with the family's yearly holiday traditions. Between her mother and her three sisters, Vernesha, Victoria and Viola, they would all rotate the holiday celebrations so that they did not bombard their mom with the task of having to do everything every holiday, every year. As their families grew, it was becoming too much for their mother to handle. She had enough on her plate with still dealing with their father, who she divorced years ago, but still took pretty good care of mostly because they never stopped loving one another. She loved her family and really enjoyed when they were able to come together like this.

She stepped off into the kitchen to check on the brewing coffee. She wanted to make sure that her guests were well-taken care, plus she knew that her mom and dad liked to sip on a hot cup of coffee while they relax after dinner. It was funny, because when she left out of the great room, they were all over each other on the dance floor. She laughed a light chuckle out loud and thought that coffee was probably the last thing on their minds at that moment.

"Inside joke?" She turned around from being frightened by the voice behind her in her kitchen. Sam apologized immediately, "Oh, I am so sorry. I did not mean to startle you." Veronica was not sure as to whom this handsome gentleman was, standing in her kitchen, but she did know that he was one of Blue's acquaintances. Blue was Victoria's man. She caught a glimpse of him, briefly at the dinner table, but she was so busy being a good hostess that she gingerly strolled by him without giving him a second glance. She was glad that she got a good look now. Mostly because he was what she would call, big and yellow.

And she liked them big and yellow. Sam was a fairly lighter-skinned, 6'3", 280 plus pounds of fine. She looked at him and thought, *Ooooo, what I could do on that man's…*

Her thought was cut off by Viola, her youngest sister, as she stepped into the kitchen. "Veronica, Dad says he wants his…" she stopped short when she noticed Sam. "Oooh, well hello. How are you doing?" Sam blushed. Viola's heat sensors went up instantly, ready to hit full-blown flirt mode until she looked at Veronica, who was giving her a "get the hell out of here" look. Viola got the hint. She smiled and said while chuckling, "Dad is waiting on his coffee, so you might want to get it out to him. Soon." Veronica smirked at her.

Viola backed out of the room slowly, but as she exited, she gave Veronica a thumbs up, pointed to Sam, who could not see her with his back was turned to her, and did a slow sensual type of dance move and mouthed the words, "You better get that, girl."

Veronica tried not to laugh, but couldn't hold it in. Sam turned around to see what was so funny and Viola straightened up and ran out of the door. He asked smiling, "Is everything okay?" Veronica was smiling also. "Yes. My sister is just a fool."

Her smile is mesmerizing. "You have such a beautiful smile," he said.

Veronica was flattered. "Why, thank you. That is so sweet of you to say." This man was making her feel some type of way. She continued, "Well, here you are standing in my kitchen, giving me sweet compliments about my smile and I have no idea as to who you are, sir." He was so taken by what was happening that he plumb forgot to introduce himself.

"How careless of me. Once again, I apologize. Samuel. Samuel Pinkerton. But everyone just calls me Sam." He reached out his hand for Veronica to take it. She reached out for a handshake but he took her hand, turned and kissed the back of it. She thought, *a gentleman. Umm, impressive.*

He released her hand and she said, "Well, I am not everyone. So nice to meet you, Samuel."

Chapter 2

Sam and Veronica really seemed to hit it off at the dinner party. They talked for about an hour at the event, but due to her hosting the party, they were not really able to get to a place of getting to know one another, before any real progress was made. Sam was very anxious to find out all that he could about this lovely lady but unfortunately, it would have to wait due to her holiday plans. She was scheduled to leave town the next morning and would be gone for the next four days. As the crowd started to decrease in size, he knew that the party was closely coming to an end. He did not want to stop talking to Veronica. He was enjoying the conversation. This woman sitting next to him was beautiful, sexy and smart. She was family oriented, but about her business as well. From her demeanor, you could instantly decipher that she was a woman of many hats. She was the oldest girl of the sisters, who sometimes had to step in to be the mother figure, sometimes even to her own mother. She ran a business out of her home, 5 days a week as a transportation freight broker, who had to sometimes take on the task of semi-truck driver, running one of the trucks within her 6-vehicle fleet. She was strong, intelligent, independent, and sexy to boot.

He knew that he wanted to get to know this woman better, so he asked, "Would it be alright if I called you when you get back in town, so that we may finish our conversation?"

Veronica liked the idea of that. This man was intriguing her interest. She replied, "Yes. That would be fine. I'd like that." She gave him her number as she watched him lock it in his phone. "Now make sure you use it," she said.

He smiled and responded, "Please believe me. I will."

Chapter 3

Veronica arrived in South Carolina early the next morning. Her son, Vernest, picked her up from the airport. She greeted her son with a big hug and a kiss. She got to the car looking for her grandchildren. "Where are they?" she asked.

Vernest said, "Well dang, Mom. I gets nothing. I can't just enjoy these five minutes with you fawning over me, for a change? Always only about the grandkids. You are cold, Ma." He laughed. She elbowed him in his side playfully and joined in on the laughter.

"Look, boy; you got your time. Love you, but I need to see my babies. Why did you not bring them with you?" He shook his head as he placed her luggage in the trunk of the car.

"Didn't want to bring them out in the cold. Besides, Ma, you know how you are."

She gave him an inquisitive look. "And that is?"

He continued, "Now you know if I would have brought them, the first thing that you would have asked was, why I brought them out in the cold."

She rolled her eyes and had to laugh at that comment, because she knew that he was right. She would have done that. She pinched him on the arm lightly and hugged his arm as he walked her to her side of the car, "Stop acting like you know me so well." They both got in the car to head to the house. She could not wait to get to her grandbabies.

Chapter 4

"Grandma!" the kids shouted and ran into Veronica's arms when she arrived.

She hugged Deon and Natasha so tight that Deon squealed, "Grandma, you are breaking me." Veronica laughed. Deon was 5 and Natasha was 8 and they were the light of Veronica's everyday existence. She tapped Deon on the bottom playfully for making that little joke.

"Boy, get out of here. I am not breaking you. I would never do that. This love is unbreakable," she laughed.

Her daughter-in-law, Tomasina, came into the foyer and greeted Veronica. "Hi, Ma." She kissed Veronica on her cheek. "Let me take your jacket," she continued. Veronica gave her, her coat, took off her shoes and put some socks on her feet from a basket next to the front door. No shoes were allowed on the carpet throughout the house, so there were always extra socks next to the door. Deon and Natasha were hanging onto Veronica's leg as she tried to walk through the house.

"Deon! Natasha! Let Grandma's leg go and let her walk in peace!" Vernest said.

Veronica looked at him and told him, "Son, they are okay."

He said, "No, Ma, they are not. Do not want them tripping you up and possibly making you fall or something like that." She understood what he was saying, so she tried to hurry up and get to the couch, so that she could just cuddle up with the kids.

She said to Deon, "What is that over there in that bag? Can you look in the bag and let me know what is in it?" Deon and Natasha ran over to the bag and saw the gifts that their grandma had obviously gotten them.

"Yay! Yay! Grandma got us a video game!" they both shouted. They ran out of the room, showing their mom what they had received.

"Ma, you do too much. They did not need those," Tomasina said.

She said, "I know, but that's what a grandma does. Besides, I don't get to see my babies that often so you know that when I come, I gift." `

Chapter 5

"How was your trip?" Sam asked. Veronica arrived back in town two days prior and was glad that Sam finally gave her a call.

"Everything was lovely," she answered. Sam waited patiently on the other end of the line as she gushed about her family, especially about her grandkids.

"Well I am so glad that you had a nice time," he said. Veronica liked the fact that he asked her about her trip and did not jump right into talking about them.

"Why, thank you, Samuel," she said. Sam was not a fan of people who called him by his full first name, because he said it made him feel old, but he had to admit that he loved the way his name rolled off of her tongue. Veronica continued, "I hope you had a lovely holiday as well. Did you get to spend time with your family?" Sam was part of a huge family and when they did holidays, they did it pretty big. His parents, siblings, his children, nieces and nephews all gathered at his favorite uncle's home for the holiday.

"Yes, I had a grand ole time," he responded. Veronica laughed because she knew that he was trying to be funny. She thought his jokes were not that funny, but she admired the fact that he tried so hard to try to impress her, that she giggled like a school girl. "I got to spend time with the kids. My daughter was in from college and my son introduced the family to the new lady in his life. Yes, we had a good time."

Veronica wanted to know more about him. The night they met, she was not looking for anything to happen with Sam, but his conversation that evening told her there was something different about this guy. She was willing to take a chance for once in her life, to see where this could go.

Sam continued, "I don't want to seem too pushy and I would love to continue this conversation about our holiday activities but to be honest, I would really love to talk more about you. Would you mind if we shift gears for a moment?" Veronica liked this, a lot. She thought, *umm, a man who was not afraid to just come out and say what he wanted, and be courteous and a gentleman at the same time.*

Sam hoped that he did not seem too aggressive, but he wasn't a man of many words when it came to what he wanted.

She responded, "Samuel, what is it you would you like to know?"

Chapter 6

Veronica was sitting at home, thinking about her evening on the night before. She and Sam were getting to know one another better and she was enjoying the time that she spent with him. It had been a little over 2 months since they started seeing each other and each day was just a little bit better than the day before. She was having the time of her life with Sam. She did not want to jinx it but she felt that this was a good move on her part. She and Sam had so much in common that it was scary. Sam came over the evening before and they had pizza for dinner and played a board game. She never spent an evening this way with a gentleman caller. The level of respect that she received was blowing her mind. He was so courteous and thoughtful in everything that he did making her feel like she was the only woman on earth that he had eyes for. Veronica was getting ready for bed when the phone rang. It was Sam. "Hello," she answered.

"Hey beautiful," Sam said. She smiled. "I just wanted to hear your voice before going to sleep for the night, so I was calling to say goodnight."

Veronica was touched by his comment. "Aww, Sam, you are such a sweetheart. I am glad that you called, because I was wishing that I could hear your voice before I went to sleep too." She felt admiration. "Thank you for granting my one wish for the evening. Goodnight, sweets."

He responded, "Goodnight, love."

Chapter 7

Sam hung up the phone with Veronica and lay in bed, thinking about how awesome he thought she was. "She has such a beautiful spirit. She is beautiful physically, and smart as a whip. She is like no other woman that I have ever met. She is making me feel things that I have never felt before. What is this feeling that is coming over me? I like this woman and I like her more than I could ever think that I could have." Sam has not had the best track record when it came to women. He was what some might call a player at heart. He did not like that term, but he had to admit he had his fair share of beautiful women. He knows that he has broken many a heart within his day, but most of the time it was not intentional. It is just that he has never met the woman who could change his mind about wanting a forever type of love and Veronica was doing something to him that was making him feel strange. Not strange in a strange way, but strange in a bizarre way. She was making him want a soulful connection. He wanted to know her emotionally and spiritually. He did not even want to rush the physical aspect of the relationship with this woman, because he respected her way too much. She made him feel alive. Sam went to sleep feeling like new money, as he always says; ready to take on a chance on the possibility of happiness.

Chapter 8

Victoria, Vernesha, and Viola were all over Veronica's house for their bi-monthly sisters' night. Ever since they were in their 20's; they would hang out at one of their houses for an entire evening and play games like Truth or Dare, Monopoly, or cards, watch a movie and have much needed heart to hearts with one another. They were always close, but this kept them in the loop of what was going on in each other's lives, because like Veronica said, "Sometimes life can get in the way of the things that really matter the most, like love, family, and friends."

Viola loved these nights because it made her feel like a grownup, she said. She got to have grownup conversations with the women in her life that she admired. There was nothing like sisters' day. Veronica was on the phone with Sam when they first arrived, so Viola could not wait to delve right in and get the dish on Sam. Viola and Vernesha, along with Veronica, were sitting on Veronica's king size bed. Victoria sat in the bedroom recliner in the corner of the room. Each of them had some type of snack in front of them. They were munching on potato chips, ice cream, doughnuts, Twinkies, cinnamon rolls, fruit, pop and mixed nuts. Viola had ordered a pizza with some wings, which were en route to be delivered. This was their night of letting themselves go and not worrying about how many calories they were going to intake, what their hair and makeup looked like, or who thought they were cute or not. While they waited for the food, Viola was lying on her stomach, legs kicked up in the air, just sitting on pins and needles and dying inside to bombard Veronica with a plethora of questions.

Viola said, "Roni, ok. What is up, sis? What is up with you and this Sam fella? You have been keeping him under tight wraps and I am ready for you to unwrap him." Victoria and Vernesha's attention perked up when Viola asked the question.

Vernesha added, "Oh my God! I've been dying to ask that question as well." Vernesha was so glad that Viola struck up this particular conversation. She jumped in, "Yeah, what is up, sis? You have been keeping this one under wraps and it is time to dish." Veronica could not help but smile when she thought of Sam.

Victoria noticed, smiled and said, "Roni, I saw that. Did y'all see that? Look at you. Oh no, Ms. Thang, you have got to tell us what is going on."

Veronica couldn't help but feel as if she had just gotten caught kissing in the back of the bleachers. She looked at her sisters, who were all giving her their undivided attention. She couldn't help but laugh as she said, "Well damn, aren't we all nosey?"

Viola said, "Yep," oh so proudly.

Veronica continued, "Things are alright. He is alright. We are just still getting to know one another. I am enjoying his company."

Viola looked at Veronica with her mouth twisted to the side and said, "You are so full of shit! You like him. We all saw your face when I brought him up. Damn, sis, come on now. I need information." Veronica knew that she could not keep anything from her sisters too long, but she was just enjoying the peace and quiet of the world of Sam and Veronica.

Vernesha said, "Come on, sis. We have not seen you like this in a long time and I like what I am seeing. You are glowing right now. Look at her, guys. She is freaking glowing."

Veronica blushed. She was having the time of her life with Sam and loved every minute of it. She said, "Guys, I like him. I like him a lot."

Viola jumped up elated, bouncing on her knees on Veronica's bed. "I knew it! I knew it! Details! Details! Details! I need details. With his big fine yellow self. I need to know everything. I know you done jumped all over big yellow fine and I need to know was it good to ya." They all laughed.

Veronica responded, "La La, you know you stupid, right?"

Viola laughed at the comment and added, "Whatever, Roni? Don't try to change the subject. I don't care what you say about me. I just wanna know what you got to say about him."

Victoria jumped in. "La La; that is none of our business." She really did want to know as well, but she tried to play as if she didn't.

. "Skip that, Vicky. I want to know too. Give up the goods, Roni", Vernesha said. Veronica proceeded to tell the girls about how she felt and what she was starting to feel, and let them know that she was in a place she has never been before and she liked it. She was a little afraid that things were moving too fast, but she was too scared to interfere with what was going on, because she felt you never know what God has in store and she was not one to block her possible blessing. She did not want to step in God's way and interfere with God's plan, she said.

Viola sat and waited patiently on the juice and Veronica never gave it up. She said, irritated but still in a joking manner, "So, you just not gonna give up the goods on big yellow, huh? I see how you do, sis. Just wrong for that. Dead wrong." She tapped Veronica on her leg gently with a love tap. Veronica knew that they were going to be shocked, because she and Sam had now made it up to 4 months within their relationship, and they had not yet succumbed to acting out their physical attraction to one another.

Veronica finally said, "I don't have anything to tell. We have not gone there as of yet."

Vernesha said, "Roni, get the fuck out of here! You are lying." Veronica said nothing. Victoria said, "You are not lying, are you?" Veronica shook her head no.

Viola sat there in shock. "Girl, you are crazy. Shit, a bitch like me? I would have jumped on the fine specimen the first night. Better be glad it was you that saw him first and not me."

Veronica spanked her on her bottom and laughed. "Girl, shut up." Victoria saw the look on Veronica's face and knew that this was something different. Her body language said it all when she mentioned his name, or spoke about him.

Victoria asked, "Sis, are you in love?" Vernesha and Viola stopped laughing, turned and while looking at Veronica, saw the seriousness in her mood. Veronica put her head down and smiled. Tears welled up in her eyes. Her sisters all looked at each other and then back to Veronica. She looked at her sisters and they saw it all over her face.

She said, "I think I am."

Chapter 9

Sam and Blue were wrapping up a business meeting. Brian Bluedell, or Blue as everyone called him, was Sam's best friend and business partner at their construction company and as of a few months ago, he was now also Victoria's husband and Veronica's brother-in-law. They were discussing the contract for a potential client within the Metro Detroit area, where they would help to build some loft-style apartments in downtown Detroit. The project was set to break ground in about 3 more weeks if things worked out. Blue was the brains and the manpower of the operation, and Sam was the one who focused more on the financial backing. Since their pairing a little over 3 years ago, they have had a very lucrative run with the many projects that have come their way. Their profit margin had nearly doubled by the second year, and they were now looking at a massive increase in profit, now that this project came along.

"Everything looks good with the numbers if you ask me. I think we should go ahead and set up a meeting with the client and begin to price the material, and try to estimate the labor cost so that we can start looking into all of the necessary permits," Blue said.

Sam really didn't get into the manual labor aspect of the deals but he really did like the numbers that he was seeing. He trusted Blue with all of the other details. He said, "What I can do is, after I have lunch with Veronica today, I can run downtown to the building permit office and apply for the necessary building permits, if you want to go ahead and look into the materials. We can look into obtaining the extra labor a little later. I would rather get these things out of the way first, especially the permits, since they can sometimes take a while to come through. Sound like a plan?"

Blue agreed and was good with that. When Sam mentioned Veronica's name, Blue wanted to shift gears just a little. He and Sam had a conversation a few weeks back, when the family gathered at their house after his son was born, and he and Victoria brought the baby home for the first time from the hospital. Sam hinted then that he was working on trying to spark something up with Veronica, but Blue was not expecting such a change in his best friend. Since their conversation, Sam seemed different. He let Sam finish his thought and then jumped right in changing the subject. "Lunch today with Veronica, huh? You two really seem to be moving forward with this thing, I see?"

Sam smiled and said, "She is great, man. I have never met anyone like her. She has this confidence about her that I like. She is strong and independent but she is still gentle enough to step back and let me be the man and I love that dude." Blue had had a conversation with Victoria after she came home the next day from their sisters' day, and she let him know what Veronica said about how she felt about Sam. Blue was curious. He just wanted to make sure that all parties were on their best behavior and that things were still going well. He was a little hesitant about Sam and Veronica in the beginning, because it was so close to home, but he liked what Veronica was doing for Sam. He liked seeing what he saw on Sam. He watched Sam, who was still smiling evidently still smiling and thinking about Veronica and for the first time in a long time, Sam seemed happy.

Chapter 10

Catrina was on her lunch break and was picking up her lunch which consisted of a deluxe Reuben sandwich, with extra pickles, and a large sweet tea. Catrina Warner was a paralegal at a law firm located just 3 blocks up the road from The Little Deli of Light, where she decided to pick up lunch from on today. As she stood there waiting for her food, she saw him. She watched him as he walked in. The last time she saw him was about a year ago. She and Sam have had an off and on thing for about almost4 years. About a year ago he became very distant, which left her a little confused by the end. He just decided one day to tell her that he was not in a place to try to get into anything serious and he felt that she wanted more than he could give her at the time. She tried to call him a couple of times after that, but he would not respond to her or return her calls. Eventually, by no choice of her own, she moved on. She watched him as he sat at a table in the corner and was tempted to head over to him and give him the shock of his life, but she decided not to at the time. She would wait to see if another opportunity would come along at a later date. And besides that, he was not alone.

Chapter 11

Veronica looked at the clock to see that it was 7:15. Dinner was almost done. She showered and dressed and put on some music. This felt like a '70s - 80s night to her, so she broke out her playlist of classic '70s – '80s tunes, which included songs by artists such as Luther Vandross, Freddie Jackson, Regina Belle, Shirley Murdock, Jermaine Stewart, Karen White, Meli'sa Morgan, Hall & Oates, Chicago, Frankie Beverly & Maze, along with so many more. She started with the smooth vocal stylings of Player's "Baby Come Back." She sat down on her white couch with a glass of white wine and closed her eyes, taking in the lyrics and singing along when the doorbell rang. She smiled and thought, *he's here.*

Chapter 12

Veronica opened the door and Sam was blown away by the vision in front of his eyes. She stood there in all-white, looking like an angel that just dropped down from heaven. Her cocoa-brown skin glowed as she greeted him with her beautiful smile. She had moisturized her body with shea butter cream and even though he was not sure as to what the exact fragrance was, he thought she smelled absolutely divine. She wore a white linen dress that softly clung to her body, showing off her amazing arms, which were the result of working out in the gym at least 3 days a week. Her hair hung down just above her shoulders, flowing when a slight gust of wind breezed through the door as she stood there, waiting for him to come in. "Hey baby," she said.

Sam entered the foyer and kissed her on the cheek. She loved that he was such a gentleman. "Hello beautiful," he greeted her.

She blushed. He was always making her blush. "May I take your jacket?" Sam removed his jacket and handed it to Veronica, who hung it in the coat closet located in the foyer. "I hope you are hungry. Dinner is almost ready."

He answered, "Starved."

Chapter 13

Sam was stuffed. He couldn't eat another bite even if he wanted to. Veronica had outdone herself with the roast, red potatoes, peas and carrots. There were homemade sweet dinner rolls, freshly squeezed lemonade, and a marble cake, with frozen yogurt topped with mixed berries to help to finish it all off. Sam sat on the couch, ready to take a nap. He said, "Roni, you have outdone yourself. Everything was delicious. I have not had a home-cooked meal like that in a very long time." Veronica thanked him and offered him some coffee. He told her that maybe he would like some coffee a little later. Veronica poured two glasses of white wine and turned the music up a little. She wanted to sit and enjoy Sam's company for a while. She sat next to him on the couch, sipped some wine and then leaned her head on his shoulder. She just wanted to be next to him. Sam shifted and moved her body so that she could lay within his arms. They both sat still, cuddled up on the couch, listening to some good music and both thinking that this was a good place to be.

Chapter 14

Veronica woke up around 1:15 am. She and Sam had both dozed off, still cuddled up on the couch. She knew that he was tired from working overtime on a work project and she did not want to wake him because he looked so well rested. She watched him sleep and thought he was just as fine asleep as he was when he was awake. She giggled as she thought about Viola calling him, "big yellow fine." *That girl is a fool, but she sure is right. This brother is fine.* She was satisfied just watching him sleep, but knew he probably was not that comfortable in the position he was sitting in. She just wanted to look at him just a little while longer, though. She lay on his chest and listened to his heartbeat and tried to imagine what it was feeling on the inside. She moved closer to him, wanting to feel the warmth of his body next to hers. When she shifted her body, she must have startled him, because he jumped slightly and woke up. He smiled when he realized where he was. He looked down at her and said, "Hi, beautiful. Good thing it wasn't just a dream this time."

She blushed. "Stop that. You are always making me blush," she said.

He reached down, lifted her face to his, kissed her gently and said, "And want to make you do so much more."

Chapter 15

"Are you sure?" Sam asked. Veronica kissed Sam once again on his lips, stood up, embraced his hand and led him to the bedroom. Veronica was a businesswoman at heart and that is what took up the majority of her time. Veronica had no type of personal life, so she did not date. The last time she dated seriously was 2 years prior to meeting Sam.

Sam wanted to respect everything that there was about Veronica, including her love life. There was a time that all he wanted to do was try to get a woman in bed with him, have a little fun and then move on to the next but with Veronica, he wanted more. He did not want to move too fast with her. He wanted it to be the right time, right day, and the right moment. He wanted to be able to make love to her. He had never wanted someone so much in his life. He waited almost 5 months for this moment and wanted to make sure that he still was not moving too fast.

Veronica knew that this was the day. She knew that he was the one. She knew that she wanted to be loved on, touched, and kissed by this man who was now standing in her bedroom with her. She wanted everything that he could give and more. She answered, "Yes, I'm sure."

Chapter 16

Veronica felt as if her skin was on fire. She wanted Sam so much. Sam wanted to take his time and explore every part of Veronica's body slowly. He began to remove her dress. He slipped the strap off of her right arm revealing one of her perky breasts. He made love to her mouth with his, while caressing her right breast with his left hand. He held her close to his body, not wanting any space in between them. He wanted to feel her next to him and never wanted to let her go. He lightly squeezed and rolled her nipple in between his index finger and thumb, making it protrude and prepared it for insertion between his lips. He kissed and sucked on it, making Veronica want more. He removed her left strap and repeated the same action, but now caressing both breasts with both hands at the same time, while taking turns placing light kisses from one to the other. He kissed her mouth, her neck, her chest. He caressed her bottom, pulling her closer and closer to his now protruding member, giving her an idea of what was in store.

Veronica stepped out of her dress and began to unbutton Sam's shirt as he continued to caress her body Veronica kissed Sam on his chest with light tender kisses. This drove him wild. The more she kissed the closer he tried to pull her into his body. Sam traced his hand slowly down the front of Veronica's body, down into her black panties and slipped his fingers inside of her. Veronica moaned and called out, "Samuel." He looked in her eyes and made love to her with his hand, enjoying every expression that showed up on her face. He watched her bite her bottom lip, revealing the pleasure that she was experiencing with every in and out movement. Veronica met each movement, gyrating against his hand wanting to finally feel his member inside of her. She kissed his mouth, introducing their tongues by letting them get to know one another better. Veronica reached down and unbuttoned his pants, then pushed them down past his buttocks. Sam wiggled them down until they hit the floor around his ankles. Veronica was so wild with anticipation that she could not wait any longer. She reached down in his boxers which were now halfway down his bottom, grabbed his member, lifted her leg slightly, removed his hand and slowly inserted it inside of her.

From the lack of physical pleasure over the two years plus, Sam wanted to be gentle with her as not to overwhelm her with the amount of his girth. He stepped completely out of his pants and boxers, lifted her leg up higher and slowly moved in and out. Veronica grunted as he opened up her sensual soft side. Sam was driven to madness from the feel of Veronica snuggled so tightly upon his member. He started out gently. In and out he moved with such precision. Her inside's grip was warm and voraciously snug. This woman was a beast. He tried so hard to take it slowly, but she was too much for him to handle. Slowly, he started to move a little faster and then a little harder. Veronica took it all, moaning from pain but mostly from pleasure. He moved a little faster and then a little harder. Veronica struggled a bit, but met each stroke wanting him to stop, but not wanting him to stop even more. He moved a little faster and then a little harder. Veronica hollered out louder and louder but needed him to never let her go. She held onto his shoulders as he pulled her into his body, pounding against her, driving deeper and deeper into her. He moved a little faster and then a little harder.

Sam looked at Veronica, wanting to make sure that he was not giving her too much, because she was giving him everything. He wanted to make sure that she was okay. He'd waited so patiently and so long for her. He could not believe that this was real and that he existed in this space. She stared into his eyes letting him know not to stop. Sam did not want to stop. He felt as if he could not stop, even if his life depended on it. He never felt anything like this before. He grunted and squeezed her bottom tightly, pulling her onto his member harder faster. The sounds of their bodies slapping together, mixed in with their sounds of being driven to pure ecstasy took over the room. And just when she thought she could not take anymore, Veronica began to shake and tremble. Sam knew that she was at the point of no return. He grabbed her bottom even tighter and pulled her into his member even faster and harder, wanting her to explode all over him. He wanted to give her what she had been waiting for. What he had been waiting for. What they both had longed for, for the past 5 months. He wanted to witness this beautiful woman he knew he was falling in love with, show him what her climactic episode looked like. What it felt like. He wanted her and he wanted to be the only one to give her this feeling for all of her days. Veronica shouted, "Samuel, it's coming, baby! It's coming, baby!" That did it. *The name*. He never thought his name was more beautifully said than when it escaped her lips at that moment. Sam lifted her up off of the ground, throwing both of her legs over his shoulders and with a tight grip on her firm soft supple bottom, slapped her body against his body even faster until he brought a roar out of her so ferocious, it sounded like a lioness protecting her cub. Sam drove her to a destination where she had never been. Veronica, breathing heavily, looked at Sam feeling tired and beat, but saw from the look in Sam's eyes, that he wanted more. Sam looked at her with seductive eyes while breathing heavily and said, "Lay down, baby. We're just getting started."

Chapter 17

It was 4:23 am. Veronica and Sam lay in each other's arms after an amazing night of lovemaking. Sam could not seem to get enough of this woman. She was amazing. He never had it so good. She made him experience a physical pleasure that he never knew was possible. He himself tried so hard not to overwhelm Veronica with a full night of pleasure, due to her not having dated or being intimate in over 2 years, but Veronica was the one who was insatiable. She also couldn't seem to get enough of this man. Veronica had never been taken to the heights of passion she had experienced tonight. Sam took her over and over again, making her want him even more after every session ended. Sam knew that she was the one from the first moment that he saw her. He knew that she could change his heart. He knew that she could change his soul. Veronica was so happy with this thing that she and Sam had going on, that she was not willing to give of herself completely before it was the right time and last night was the right time. She wanted to know him personally and spiritually before releasing her body to him. She knew that Sam would be the one who was to get her to let go of all of her inhibitions. They lay together thinking the same thoughts at the same time and finally fell asleep, looking forward to the moment when they would finally wake up for the first time, intertwined within each other's arms.

Chapter 18

Catrina sat at her dining room table eating a bowl of cereal, watching the news while her cat rubbed against her ankle, meowing under the table. She had a long day and all she wanted to do once she got home from work was take a bath, eat a bowl of cereal and fall asleep while reading a good book. It had been a crazy week. She worked as a paralegal, along with 2 others for a team of tax lawyers. That time of year was coming up when they were going to be working countless hours, trying to keep up with the many issues dealing with everything plausible when it comes to clients and dealings with the Internal Revenue Service. Purvis, her cat, who'd earned his name from his constant purring, nestled and purred at her feet. She grabbed a handful of his treats from the container located at the edge of the counter and placed them on the floor next to him. "Here, love. Mommy got a little treat for you. You know you know how to beg, don't you?" she smiled. She rubbed his head. Purvis was happy.

After she finished her bowl of cereal, she shut off the television and headed to bed. She grabbed her book from off of the nightstand and turned on the clock radio to play a little mood music as she read. As she read her book, Sam Cooke's "Bring it on Home to Me" began to play in the background. Once the DJ announced the artist's name,

Catrina's mind was immediately put on Sam. She thought about him and wondered how, but more particularly, what he was doing. She wondered who the woman was that she saw him with a couple of days prior. Not like she really cared because her motto was, "You are single until the day you put a ring on that finger at the church or at the courthouse." If you were not married, you were fair game, so she decided—what the hell? Catrina reached over, grabbed her cell phone off of the dock where it was sitting and scrolled through her contacts to find his phone number which was listed as, "Pinky." She hit send.

Chapter 19

Sam did not recognize the phone number. It had been a while since he and Catrina had had any dealings with one another, and he'd never transferred her number to his new phone once he purchased it a few months back. He answered, "Hello?" She was always turned on by the bass in his voice.

"Well, hello there, stranger."

Sam was not sure who this woman was on the other end of the line. It was now 11:41 pm and over the past 5 months, the only person that really called him around this time of night would have been Veronica, so he was more than lost as to who this woman was.

"Excuse me?" he responded. It had been well over a year since he and Catrina had spoken. "Who is this?" he asked.

Catrina had an attitude, she felt as if he was supposed to know who she was. "Oh, it's like that? You don't even recognize my voice anymore?" she said.

Sam was still not sure who he was talking to. He was starting to get a little irritated. "Who is this? Don't have time to play the guessing game." She thought it was a little funny that he was getting angry. "Dang, don't bite my head off," she laughed. "Tell you what. I will give you a little clue. Imagine me whispering in your ear, Take that shit, daddy."

Sam knew. "Catrina?" he called out, hesitantly.

She giggled, "In the flesh, baby."

Chapter 20

Viola was on the line screaming with excitement, "Aaaaaah! Okay, girl, tell me was it everything?" Veronica shook her head and laughed. "I am not going to give you the details, but I have never felt anything like it ever before. The experience was," she paused, "mind-blowing." She could not stop smiling.

Viola screamed again. "I knew it! That's what the fuck I'm talking about! You better get it, sis!" she said. All four sisters were on a conference call when Veronica depicted for them some details of her night with Sam. She did not describe specifics but one thing was for sure, she knew that she would never see Sam the same way again after their night together.

Vernesha asked, "So how are you feeling about it? I mean, what does this mean for you two? Do you see yourself moving further within your romantic relationship?"

Victoria interjected, "Because, I know that you really like him. I can hear the smile all in your voice." Victoria was right. Veronica did have the biggest smile on her face. She was happy and if her sisters could see her, they would see it dripping all over her. She said, "I don't know. But he seems to be happy. At least, I hope he's happy. I know that I am happy. I have never been this happy with a man before. I like him so much. All I know is that I don't want this feeling to end. I don't want it to go away," she answered.

There was a moment of silence on the line and then Vernesha commented, "Roni, you're in love."

Without her sisters knowing it, a single tear ran down Veronica's cheek and this time she knew for sure. She responded by agreeing with Vernesha, "Yeah, Sis, I am."

Another moment of silence and then Viola said, "Hot damn! Sam done came, popped that cherry, turned big Sissy out and done made that heifer fall in love! Like Ms. Sophia said, 'I know'd they's a God.'" They all fell out with laughter.

Veronica said, still laughing, "Get off my line, fool!"

Chapter 21

Sam decided to meet up with Catrina for lunch. She'd called and told him how she was having an issue with a water leak in one of her rooms in her condo, located in the Orange Blossom Condominiums. She was calling him to see if he could come by to see what the damage would cost to have it repaired. Sam wanted to send Blue or one of the staff over to check it out, but she insisted that she needed for him to do it. He knew that it wasn't a good idea when she asked, but he went ahead and told her that he would stop by during his lunch break today. They were on 6 days for the time being, so it was Saturday and Catrina was off for the day. She told him that she would fix him a little something to eat at the house, if he could do her the favor of swinging by at around noon.

Sam arrived about 10 minutes early. When he got to the door, he could smell that she was cooking some chicken. Catrina was not what he thought of as wife material, because she was a bit too pushy, too aggressive and too much of a party girl, but she had some special skills in the bedroom that any man would appreciate and she was also one hell of a cook. Sam came to the door on his P's and Q's, because he knew what Catrina wanted. It was what she always wanted. Him. Horny, naked and double downing on her wet hot spot, as she always said. She was always trying to get with him. He decided to depart from her life a year ago and has not seen her since, so when she called the other night, he was a little shocked to say the least. He really had not thought about her in a long time. He rang the doorbell.

"Coming," Catrina said. She opened up the door and Sam knew that this was most definitely a very bad idea.

Chapter 22

When Catrina knew that Sam was going to be stopping by, she knew that she needed to step up her game. She watched Sam with that woman, who was absolutely gorgeous, at the Deli a few days before and could tell that he was really into her. She could see that there was something different about him. It showed in the way he stood, the way he laughed, the way he looked and the way he looked at her. Sam was the one that she always thought would always be around. They had been in an off and on type of romantic friendship for years. They had so much fun together when they hung out. She never let him know it, but he sensed that she always hoped that their relationship would progress into something more. Unfortunately, he always seemed to be so distant when it came to matters of the heart. He would be there one minute and then would be really standoffish the next. She tried not to think about him that way, but she liked who she was when she was with him. She felt as if he made her want to be a better person. She partied a little less when he was around. She did not drink or smoke as much either. She cut off her other male friends whenever he came around, because she did not need anyone else; making love to Sam was like making love to a 100 men at once. The way he stroked, licked, sucked and moved within her walls was enough to drive any woman mad. *And his member.* She could imagine it in her hands, between her lips and between her legs. She felt the moisture developing between her legs, just thinking about it. She missed him. She missed him so much, that on that particular morning, she went out and did a little shopping to get a few articles of clothing she knew would entice him just a little or at least make him think about the good times, so when she opened the door and saw the look on Sam's face, she knew that she had picked a winner. *Round one, Catrina 1, Sam 0. Game on.*

Chapter 23

"Please, come in," Catrina said. Sam stepped inside the door. He knew that he should make an excuse right away, so that he could get out of there as soon as possible because when he saw Catrina, his member did a dance. A dance for joy. It wanted to do the tango. The lambada. Some *Dirty Dancing*. It didn't want to back Baby in a corner, but it wanted Baby to back that thang up. She was wearing a snug, fit yellow crop top T-shirt, revealing her flawless hourglass-shaped mid-section with no bra, nipples erect on her size-D breasts, which sat up perfectly and seemed as if they were calling out to him. Her hips and bottom were filling out a pair of white fleece pants, showing the results of the many hours that she spent in the gym, trying to perfect her already perfect body. Catrina had the body of a goddess and she knew it; she knew how to make it work for her when she wanted what she wanted and at this time, he knew that she wanted him.

Sam said, "Thank you. I wanted to make sure that I got by here today, because next week will be a killer as far as free hours will be concerned." He was trying to say anything to distract her thoughts and his too. She was looking at him like a pork chop in a dog kennel. He lied, "And I just got a call from Blue, wanting to see if I may be able to cut my lunch hour short, to get back to the office to go over some financials, while we have a free moment today." Catrina knew that he was lying and all it was doing was turning her on. She knew that he was still attracted.

She responded, "Sorry to hear that," with a smirk on her face. "But hopefully you at least have enough time to eat a little something." She gave him a seductive glance and continued, "At least something with some sustenance."

Sam was thinking that he needed to get out of there now but said, "I should have enough time for a quick sandwich or something after I see the room."

She laughed because she knew that he knew better than that and said, "Now, come on. I don't see you for a little over a year and you think that I would let you come over and eat a sandwich. You know you smell something more. Yeah, right, a measly sandwich." Sam had to admit that the house smelled lovely. Catrina could put it down in the bedroom but in the kitchen, she was top chef.

"It does smell good in here, Catrina. You have always been an excellent cook. What are we having, may I ask?" he said.

She looked at him and said, "Whatever you want, but as far as food is concerned, I pan fried some skinless, boneless chicken breasts, steamed broccoli and asparagus, some homemade macaroni and cheese and made some real strawberry banana fruit smoothies. I thought I would go mostly healthy, due to the fact that you have to go back to work, but I had to do my mac and cheese for you because I know how much you love it." She was right. Her macaroni and cheese was to die for. The best he had ever had. He hadn't had Veronica's as of yet but for now, Catrina had that one in the bag. Sam tried to ignore the first part of her response and kept on task. He clapped his hands and rubbed them together and said, "Can we see the room now? I would like to get back to that mac and cheese. The smell is calling my name." She led the way while thinking the whole while, *and when I get you in this room, hopefully, I will be too.*

Chapter 24

Saved by the bell, Sam thought when he heard his cell ring. He saw the caller, smiled and answered, "Hey you."

Veronica was on the other end of the phone. "Hey, handsome. Got a minute?" she asked. Sam excused himself out of the room and stepped out onto Catrina's patio. He closed the door behind him. He was so glad that Veronica called, because Catrina was coming on strong and he was starting to weaken. She had cornered him the room and was trying her best to get to him by seducing him and as much as he hated to admit it, she was winning this chess game. She kept bending over in front of him to show him the damage the leak had done to the floorboards. While doing this, she rubbed her bottom across his member at least 3 times. She did it again 2 more times by stepping in between him and the doorway, leaving in and out of the room. She lifted her arms, showing him the damage to the ceiling, revealing the bottom cleavage of her braless breasts. Once she lifted up so far, she revealed one of her nipples. Sam was holding out for now, but Sam was just a man a virile man at that. Catrina, felt his protruding member after she brushed up against him the last two times; knowing Sam was moved, she went for the gusto. She tried to place her hand down Sam's pants, but he backed off from her reach before she had a chance to touch him. She was being a temptress and he was almost so tempted, he was just about ready to rip off her clothes and give her what she was asking for, by throwing her against the wall and taking her from behind, right there in that water damaged room.

That was when the phone rang. Thankful that he was snapped back into his reality, he said, "All the time in the world for you, beautiful." Veronica loved when he called her beautiful. He was a man who realized it is just the little things that make the most difference to a woman.

She smiled. "Want to come over tonight? I was thinking of making a big ole pot of goulash and inviting the sisters over with their honeys and making it a couples' night. I like to try to get them away from the brats from time to time and let them have some grown-up time. We can play some games, chit chat, catch up or whatever." Sam was thinking about what she said, so he said, "Couples' night? So we a couple now?" he asked.

Veronica was thrown for a loop. She was not sure as to what she should say next. She did not want to say yes and then scare him off, but she did not want to say no and then make him feel unwanted, because she was sure that she wanted him. She said, trying not to sound unsure, "I mean, is that alright? I would like to think we are, or at least I would like for us to be, but only if that is okay with you?"

He sure as hell was okay with it. "I am more than okay with that," he said. They were both smiling from ear to ear. "I would love to come by tonight and help you host the gathering, since we are now a couple. Would that be alright with you?" he asked.

She smiled and said, "I would love that."

He knew what he had to do. "Okay babe, I am wrapping up a meeting here with a client, but I will see you when I get off, okay? Bye, love."

Veronica said, "Bye."

Chapter 25

Catrina was pissed. Sam got a phone call and she assumed that it must have been that woman, because he excused himself and went outside to take the call. He came back in and made up some lame ass excuse, and asked if he could fix a plate to go and he left. After she closed the door behind him, she said, "Damn! I had that ass. Cocked and ready to shoot off that bullet and then this bitch called." She giggled, "That's alright, though. 'Til next time. I'll get that ass next time."

Chapter 26

Veronica loved her sisters with all of her heart. She cherished their relationship, especially their friendship. After Victoria's bad accident, where she and Blue were run off the road, then turned out to be okay and the baby survived, Veronica decided that she wanted to do more with the family. She realized life is too short to not enjoy every moment of it there is. This scenario was all new for Sam and Veronica, so this was going to be an interesting night. They had all gathered, ate dinner and were now sitting in the living room, playing games. They were having a good time laughing, drinking, and enjoying each other's company. They all came to play and they all came to win.

Viola was the only one without a date, so she brought her best friend, Luciano, with her along to the party. She and Luciano had been friends since they were 7, so if she was to play competitive games with anyone, it would be him, because he knows her like no other and she in turn, knew him as well. Viola was completely unaware, but Luciano was secretly in love with her since high school, but never said anything for fear of wrecking their friendship. So, he just sat back and watched her make mistake after mistake, with guy after guy over the years. He took what he could get and loved her from afar.

Vernesha and her husband, Antonio, were so hyped. They don't get a chance to really get away from their 3 kids that often for some grown-up time, just the two of them, so they were extremely amped up about the event, strategizing and giving each other high-fives every time they got an answer right.

, Victoria and Blue were newlyweds and new parents, .so they were still in that honeymoon stage of not really knowing what it feels like not to be able to get away for some me time, so they were the most casual of all.

Viola chimed in, "Okay. Okay. We have played Scrabble and Jenga," she looked at Luciano and said, "And whipped that ass on that Scrabble, did we not, boo?" She laughed while snapping her fingers. "But anyway, let's turn up the heat a little bit. Let's play Truth or Dare."

Luciano jumped up and was like, "No! Hell no! I wants no part of that game. That shit gets you in trouble, man." Everyone agreed with Luciano.

Viola said, "Y'all a bunch of punks. Come on. We're all grown. We all have taken a couple of knocks across our heads from time to time. We are all family, so there is nothing I think anyone in this room would say that would change that. At least, I know I don't have nothing to hide." The sisters and Luciano all looked at one another, paused and then burst out laughing. Blue also had to chuckle too at that comment. Sam was new to the crew, but could tell that she was a little full of it too, though. Viola said, "What? What are y'all laughing at? What's so damn funny?" The sisters and Luciano all cut in separately.

Luciano said, "The time I said that you were getting a little chunky in the butt, after you asked me about it and I gave you the truth, you did not talk to me for three and a half weeks."

Victoria cut in, "Vernesha, remember when we told her that that guy, Quan, was no good for her and that he was just using her for her car by dropping her off at work and running around in her car all day? And then on top of that, he was picking her up late from work almost every day?"

Vernesha jumped in, "Oh, and but wait…then, she would call one of us to come to pick her up and then try to tell us not to say anything about him on the topic, because it was her man and her business." She looked at Viola. "But your ass sitting in the passenger seat of my car."

Viola stuck her middle finger up at Vernesha and mouthed the word, "Bitch." Vernesha laughed with a look of shock on her face.

Veronica said, "La La you have to admit, you really don't want to play this game. You are one that does not like to hear the truth." They were all still laughing.

Viola stood up, looked all of them up and down and said, "Man, fuck y'all!" She joined in on the laughter. "Come on, let's play the damn game."

Chapter 27

"Sam, Truth or Dare?" Viola had scanned the room for her next victim. She decided that she was going in on Sam. He was having a great evening, spending time with Veronica's family. He never was so involved with a woman that he was dating. He'd never met anyone's family before. The interaction was something he never really thought about. He was glad Veronica wanted to do this.

He said, "Truth. Come on, what you got for me?"

Viola said, "Okay. I see you. Sam got some balls over there." Veronica was nervous for Sam, as well as for herself. She knew her sister and there was no telling what was going to come out of her mouth. Viola saw the look on Veronica's face, and even though Veronica was showing that she was a little embarrassed and worried about what question she was about to possibly ask, she was paying more attention to Sam. The way he was looking at her sister, trying to comfort her because he saw, that she was worried. Viola saw that he was trying to take care of her because he noticed that Veronica needed to be taken care of. She looked over to Victoria and Vernesha, who noticed it too. She had a juicy question for him too, but her seeing their interaction together changed her mind. Viola looked at them both and saw it all over both of their faces.

She looked over at Vernesha once again, who smiled and shook her head in agreement, because she already knew what the question was going to be and asked, "Truth? Are you in love with my sister?" already knowing the answer.

Veronica looked up at her shocked and even more embarrassed that Viola had asked that question. Sam took Veronica's hand, placed his other hand on cheek, turned her face towards him, looked her in her eyes and said, "Yes."

Chapter 28

Veronica never knew that she could be this happy. She moved her body slowly on top of Sam's member, with her hands sitting firmly in the middle of his chest, bracing her every move as she gave him the love that she felt inside. She slid up and down on it while he met her body, feeling the warmth of her insides. She began to move faster and rode him, moaning with pleasure, until she climaxed while calling out his name. But he was not done. He lifted her hips slightly and moved his body upwards into her inner sanctum until she began to once again come down on top of him slowly. Sam loved this woman so much. He never wanted her to leave his side, because he knew that she was the one. He knew what he had to do and what he wanted to say—what he had to say. Sam looked her in her eyes and said, "Marry me?"

She leaned down and made love to his mouth while he held her hips, helping to guide her up and down on him, until he could not take it anymore. He released inside of her, spreading his love within her walls, wanting to be so close to her that they would become one.

Chapter 29

Catrina tried calling Sam a few times within the past few days. He would not return her phone calls, but kept texting her to get in touch with his business partner and they would be happy to have someone come over to finish looking at the job for her. She did not want anyone else other than him to come over. She saw that she was going to have to step up her game. She realized it had to be this chick that was messing everything up. Her plans were being ruined. She needed to find out who this chick was, because she was starting to get on her nerves. But how?

Chapter 30

Sam and Veronica decided to meet for lunch. Veronica really enjoyed the Deli that he took her to a couple of weeks before, so she decided to meet him there once again. They had the best raspberry tarts that she had ever tasted. Sam opened the car door for Veronica when she arrived. He kissed her on the lips and they walked hand in hand into the Deli. They chose a table up front in the corner next to the window, overlooking the man-made pond just outside the restaurant. They sat at the table staring into each other's eyes with their hands intertwined, having a pleasant conversation about their day and their plans for later on that evening.

Catrina sat in the car just down the street and waited for her lunch hour to be over.

Chapter 31

Veronica stopped on her way home by the beauty supply store to grab some of her favorite hair products. She had plans on doing her monthly grooming routine over the weekend, which included a deep conditioning ritual that helped to keep her hair shiny and healthy looking. Viola was hairdresser to all the sisters, but Veronica would do some of these things at home, because going to Viola's shop could be very time consuming, if she had to do it all. Viola's clientele list was enormous and you could be there for hours before she was even able to get your hair washed and dried. As she strolled the aisle, she was approached by a woman who started asking her about the product that she was placing in her hand basket. "Excuse me?" Catrina said. "Can you recommend a good beauty product that I can try to make my hair look like yours? Your hair is beautiful." Even though Catrina was clearly wearing a weave, she went ahead and told her about some of her favorites. Catrina went on say that she wanted to make a change and start wearing her natural hair, because she was tired of the hassle of having to constantly go to her hairdresser to maintain her hairstyle.

Veronica said, "These products are my faves. They have jojoba oils, which are good for your skin, scalp and revitalize your hair follicles to help promote healthy hair growth and full shiny hair." Catrina was sizing Veronica up the entire time that she was talking. *She was gorgeous, I'll give her that, but she's not me,* she thought.

She was going on and on about the hair products and Catrina was thinking that she couldn't care less about anything this chick was talking about, but she needed to know more information. Catrina said, "My man also says that he wants to run his fingers through my hair without hitting a track, so I need to do something." She laughed. Veronica thought that this conversation was taking a turn and she was not interested in it at all. She tried to laugh it off and started to continue to search the aisle for one last product. Catrina could tell that she was trying to get away from her. "I know your man doesn't have any complaints. Look at you. You are stunning."

Veronica was really feeling uncomfortable. All she wanted to do was find the hot oil treatment and get away from this lady, who was being strange. "Thank you for the compliment. You are a very beautiful woman yourself," she responded.

Catrina was thinking, *bitch, I know that.*

Veronica found the hot oil treatment. "Well, got what I needed. It was very nice talking to you. I hope that the products work out for you as well as they do for me." Veronica started walking down the aisle, trying to get away from this woman as fast as she could. Catrina gave a sinister smile as she watched Veronica pretty much sprint down the aisle trying to escape from her, and said oh-so-slyly, "Yeah, thanks. I am pretty sure that they will work great and Sam Pinky will love the results it provides for my hair as well. Have a good one." Veronica stopped short. She went to turn around and said, "Did you say Sam Pink…" but Catrina was gone.

Chapter 32

Veronica searched the store looking for Catrina. By the time she realized where she was, she was pulling out of the parking lot in her red Mercedes. She stood there outside the store watching Catrina's car race out of the parking lot, confused and wondering what the hell had just happened. She finally let herself go. She finally opened up her heart. She finally found someone she thought that she could trust and now this? Was Sam not who she thought he was? Was Sam not being loyal and faithful to her? Who was this woman and why did she leave before even paying for any of her products? They were left in her basket on the floor of the aisle and so were a pair of keys with a key chain which read, "Orange Blossom Condominiums."

Chapter 33

Catrina felt such a rush as she headed towards I-96 East. She had been having her lunch hour for the past week in her car, sitting down the street from the Deli hoping that she would luck up and spot Sam and his little lady friend and today, it had paid off. She felt that she did enough damage to make waves within whatever crock of bull that Sam had going on with that chick. She wanted Sam. She had waited on him. Had been waiting on him for years to come around finally and choose her over all of the bitches that he had and she thought that she was going to just let him go that easily. No, that was not going to happen. She was going to just wait this out. Once the beautiful, stuck-up princess got the fight started and kicked him out of her life, he would come running back to her like he always does. He always comes back to her. Always. She pulled in her driveway after the 10-minute drive, exited her car and began to search for her keys. She could not find them. She was in such a rush; she did not realize that she dropped them in the basket when she dipped out of the aisle at the beauty supply. She thought, *maybe I left them in the house.* She called the HOA to contact maintenance to let her in.

Chapter 34

Veronica called her sisters to find out what to do. Viola, who was always down for a Detroit beat down was all but ready to go and find this girl. Veronica has too much class for such crude behavior, so that is not what she was inclined to do.

Victoria asked, "Well, have you talked to Sam about it?"

Veronica did not know what to do. "No, I haven't contacted him yet. She did not say his whole name, but there is no way she could not have been talking about him. How many 'Sam Pinky's,' as she called him, would be running around here? I don't know what to do."

Viola said, "Beat that ass! Hers and his!"

Vernesha said, "Shut the hell up, La La! You always trying to start trouble!"

Viola retorted, "Why am I the one starting trouble? This bitch runs up on my sister and tried her! I wanna beat that hoe's ass! This shit ain't got nothing to do with Sam. This all has to do with my big sis. She won't fight, but I will."

Victoria said, "La La, calm down. This is Veronica's fight, not yours." She addressed Veronica, "Roni, what are you thinking?" Veronica was silent. Her mind was in overdrive. Victoria sensed that she was not sure what to say. "Sis, personally, I think you need to call Sam and let him know what happened."

Veronica knew that Victoria was right. "I know, Vicky. I know. But I am scared that I may find out something that I just don't want to know."

Chapter 35

Sam arrived at Veronica's at 6:45 pm. He did not go home. He always kept extra clothes in the car on a just in case he went straight to Veronica's after work, so he would just shower and get dressed when he got there. Most of the time, he just showered and the clothes would instantly become optional. He came straight in because when she knew he was coming, she would leave the door unlocked for him. He walked in and found her sitting in the kitchen on a stool at the island. He kissed her on the cheek, but she moved away as soon as his lips touched her face. Sam stood back and watched her and he saw her body language was saying that something was on her mind. "Is everything alright, babe?" he asked.

Veronica took the keys that were clutched tightly in her hands and threw them on top of the island. Sam watched them slide across the surface space. He picked them up, looked at her confused and said, "What is this?"

Veronica said, "You tell me?"

Sam was lost. "Babe, what are you talking about? Whose keys are these? And why are you obviously angry with me about them?"

Veronica was lost at this time too. It seemed as if he was just as confused by this as she was. She said, "I was approached today by a woman in the beauty supply store, who was acting very strange, asking me questions and saying the most inappropriate things to me." She stopped, waiting to see if she would get any type of reaction out of him. He gave her nothing.

Sam waited for her to finish. He said, "Okay? And what pray tell, does that have to do with me? Who was she?"

Veronica was starting to feel a little foolish. "Sam, I want to be able to trust you and all, but if you are seeing someone else, this is not going to work out. I am too fragile to deal with something like that. I did not open myself up to you for you to screw with my heart. I can't take that," she said.

Sam put the keys back down on the island, walked over to Veronica, grabbed both of her hands looked her in her eyes and said, "Are you fucking kidding me? Babe, what the hell is going on? Girl, do you know I love the ground that you walk on? But I am so damn confused right now. What happened? Why do you think that I am seeing someone else and how could I when I have been with you every single night?" Veronica knew that he was right, but the stranger calling his name, is what threw her off. She took a deep breath and told him the story about her encounter with the strange lady. Sam listened and knew who it was. The red Mercedes with the personal license plate was a dead giveaway. He picked up the keys and noticed the name on the key ring, Orange Blossom Condominiums. They had a long talk about his past relationship with Catrina whereas he explained everything. He was livid because now, she was messing with his future. He said with vengeance in his voice, "Come on, babe. She wants to know who you are, let's inform her. Let go for a ride."

Chapter 36

Sam sent a text message to Catrina, asking if she was at home and if he could stop by. Catrina got excited when she saw the message. She replied that he was welcome to come by. She hopped in the shower, threw on some sexy underwear and a skimpy pair of shorts with a sports bra and waited for him to arrive. It was around 9:30, so she knew that this had nothing to do with business. She was absolutely clueless as to why he was really stopping by, so she was ready for a night of hot sex and multiple orgasms. In her rush to leave the beauty supply store earlier that day, she did not notice Veronica standing in the glass door of the beauty supply, watching her as she pulled out of the parking lot in her red Mercedes with the license plate that read, "HOT Lik FRE."

Chapter 37

Catrina told Sam that the door would be unlocked and to let himself in, and that she would be in the bedroom watching some television. Twenty minutes later, Sam entered the apartment. He stepped in first and wanted to make sure that Catrina did not see Veronica enter the apartment along with him. He saw that she was in the bedroom as she stated, because it was the only illumination of light throughout her home, besides the light shining from the kitchen from the over the stove light. He gestured for Veronica to follow behind him. Sam headed towards the bedroom. Catrina heard him come in. "Is that you, Sam?" she asked. He did not answer. He cut the corner and there she lay on her stomach, head propped up on a pillow with her butt cleavage showing beneath the edge of her tiny shorts, watching a reality television show. She turned to look at him. "What a surprise to hear from you tonight. The way that you have been ignoring my phone calls and trying to send your business associates over to check out the room,

I thought that maybe you did not want anything to do with me anymore," she gloated.

Veronica was not into violence, but she wanted to come around that corner and slap this little bitch right in the face, but she was patient and waited for her future husband to tell her the right moment to appear. Sam said, "No, baby girl. Just needed it to be the right moment. You know how we do." She did. He continued, "So how was your day today? Do anything special? Meet any interesting people?" Sam felt like messing with her.

Catrina was not interested in talking. She wanted this man. He was looking and smelling good. She could tell that he had no underwear on under his sweatpants from the way his massive member swung when he moved. "Come on, Sam, now I know that you did not come over here at this time of night to talk." She got off of the bed and walked towards Sam and began to remove her shorts, revealing the teal colored thong that she was wearing. She did a spin to show him what he had been missing. "Missed all of this, didn't you?" she asked.

Sam ignored her and her question and said, "Well, I just wanted to stop by because I think that I have something that belongs to you."

Catrina walked up to him and started to reach for his member and said, "You sure do." He moved away quickly and dropped her keys on the floor. Catrina looked down to the floor and was confused. She bent over and picked up her keys and asked, "How did you get these? I was looking for them today, because I was locked out of my house." She thought she had them earlier, but once she got back home and saw that she did not, she was convinced they were in the house somewhere. So, how in the heck did Sam end up with them?

Sam said, "Oh no, I can't take the credit for those."

She was starting to get irritated. "Sam, stop playing. How did you end up with my keys?" she asked. He turned to the side, now talking to Veronica, "Baby?"

Veronica stepped around the corner and said, "He didn't end up with them. I did. You know, from when you left them at the store earlier."

Catrina became afraid and ran to the other side of the room behind her bed, and snatched up the blanket off of it to cover up her half-naked body. "What the? Who the? Sam, why in the hell did you bring this bitch in my house?" she yelled.

Veronica went to step forward, but Sam stopped her and corrected Catrina before she could make another move. "Hold the hell on, now! She ain't nobody's bitch! And since you made such a big effort to try to figure out who she is, let me be the one the one to tell you. She is my fiancée. You hear that?" He pointed at Veronica. "She," he paused, "is my fiancée. The woman is to be my wife, something that you will never be and would have never been, even if she wasn't. So, my fiancée and I would like for you to make sure that you stay the hell away from both of us before you regret the day that you ever walked into our lives." Veronica was ready to pounce when Catrina called her out of her name, but evidently, it was unnecessary. Her man had her back 150 percent and she loved it.

Catrina said, "Get out, you crazy ass muthafuckas! Get the hell out of my house!"

Sam said, "Gladly. Let's get out of here, babe." Sam grabbed Veronica's hand and turned to head out of Catrina's bedroom.

Before departing, Veronica laughed and said, "Thank you for the invite. It was so nice to meet you, sweetie. Love the drapes!"

Sam looked at her and laughed. "Bring your crazy ass on, silly."

They exited Catrina's house, both laughing and headed to the car, where Sam opened Veronica's door for her to get in. Before she got in, she kissed him, looked at him and said, "Oooo, you gonna get it when we get home." Sam quickly helped her in the car, ran around and hopped in the driver's seat and headed to Veronica's. He never drove so fast in his life.

Chapter 38

Sam and Veronica had their first real test that evening and survived it with flying colors. Veronica felt like the luckiest woman on earth. She knew that she had a man by her side who was willing to go to the ends of the earth for her. She lay in his arms, listening to his breathing while he slept, closed her eyes and said a silent prayer:

Dear God,

I first would like to give you all of the honor for allowing me to stay within your presence on this earth just one more day. I come to you humbly and gratefully, for I know that without you, there is no me. God, only you know what kind of pain and hurt that I have been through and how rough it has been, and how tough it is for me to let someone in. You allowed me to see that there is not all bad in the world when it comes to love. You made it possible for me to love again. You made it possible for me to trust again. You made it possible for me to feel whole for the first time in my life. God, I thank for allowing this man to come into my life and love me the way that he loves me. I thank you for allowing me to be the one that was chosen to give my love to him. This is a love that I never even thought that I was good enough to deserve, but you saw fit for me to have something that even I was incapable of seeing. And oh God, I thank you for giving him the option of asking me to be his wife. God, he wants me to be his wife. And that's why I also thank you and bless your name for giving me the power of saying, yes.

God from the bottom of my still beating heart, I thank you. Amen

Veronica fell asleep, resting on Sam's chest and dreaming about the day that she would be able to call herself Mrs. Veronica Vassar-Pinkerton.

Chapter 39

Tonight, Sam and Veronica were hosting another game night with the couples in the family. They have been going strong for a little over a year now and have decided to get married next spring in a tropical wedding. Sam had all but moved all of his belongings to Veronica's, but had not officially moved in as of yet. She said that she did not believe in shacking up, so she would not let him live with her completely until after they were married. They spent every single night lying together in each other arms, either at her place or at his. For now, it worked for him but he could not wait until the day that he would be able to say that her home was officially their home. Tonight was a little different. All of the families were together; her siblings and her parents, his siblings and his parents. There was no Truth or Dare tonight, especially with their parents being there, but there was a whole lot of fun.

He watched Blue and Victoria, who always seemed to be hugged up as if they could not get enough of touching one another. He watched his parents, who had been married for 40-plus years and had their share of ups and downs, but still managed to love one another despite of it. He watched Veronica's parents, Mr. and Mrs. Vassar, for she never changed her name, flirting with one another, him making her smile as only he can. He watched Viola and Luciano, who were playing a friendly game of love tag with one another, laughing and giggling and clearly seeing that even though Luciano did not think it, they all noticed how he truly felt about Viola. Everyone knew this of course except Viola, who was completely blind to the fact. He looked across the room at the woman he loved; Veronica, the woman who changed his life. Because of her, he spent more time getting to know his own family. He spent more time getting to know himself. He spent more time getting to know God. She made him who he was. He watched everyone and thought for once, he truly knew what it felt like to feel like he was at home.

Chapter 40

Luciano sat next to Viola, while she talked on the phone with her new boy toy of the week. He listened to her fake giggling with the fake persona she would sometimes put on to try to impress a boy and felt that it should have made him sick, but it didn't. Luciano loved everything there was to know about Viola, so even her fakeness made him weak. He and she had been friends since the second grade. They played freeze tag, hide-n-seek, hide and go get it, kickball, softball, went to the Boys & Girls Club, and did so many more things during their years of coming up together. He never looked at her as more than a sister until they got into high school. It happened in the 10th grade, in band class, when one of their mutual friends started talking about her in a way that he had never talked about or even thought about her before. He started looking at her differently from that day forward. The older they got, the more he noticed her becoming a woman. Then one day, he became attracted to her and his feelings started to change; they haven't turned back since. He falls in love with her more and more each day. So now, he sits here, yet once again, listening to the woman he has loved more than half of his life, talking to another loser. If only he had the guts to let her know. Until then, he will just sit back and love her from afar, while sitting right by her side.

Also, see other publications by Lette

V is for Victoria: A Day in the Life of Them Vassar Girls Series Novel (Book I/ Volume I)

https://www.amazon.com/gp/product/B01N236UVL/ref=series_rw_dp_sw

V is for Veronica: A Day in the Life of Them Vassar Girls Series Novel (Book II/ Volume II)

https://www.amazon.com/gp/product/B01NBX9Q0F/ref=series_rw_dp_sw

V is for Viola: A Day in the Life of Them Vassar Girls Series Novel (Book III/ Volume III)

https://www.amazon.com/dp/B01MUOW0FH

Betrayed by Love Adored by Lies – An Anthology

http://olebigheadlette.com/betrayed-by-love-adored-by-lies-an-anthology

Follow Lette at the following Social Media Sites

Twitter - https://twitter.com/AuthorLette

Facebook - https://www.facebook.com/AuthorLette/

Goodreads - https://www.goodreads.com/author/show/16337516.Lette

Amazon - https://www.amazon.com/-/e/B06VX4XWHV

BookBub - https://www.bookbub.com/authors/lette

Or visit her on her website at www.olebigheadlette.com where her

Writing Motto is: Sharing with the world the stories that develop within this big ole head of mine!

Made in the USA
Columbia, SC
15 July 2017